Writing in Asia Series

DROUGHT

Iwan Martua Dongan Simatupang was born in 1928 in Sibolga, north Sumatra. He took part in the 1945 to 1949 Indonesian Revolution against the Dutch, and was captured in March 1949. After the Revolution, he studied medicine in Surabaya, anthropology and drama in Holland, and philosophy in Paris. He returned to Indonesia in 1961. Shortly after his return, he completed *Ziarah* (Jakarta, 1969) which was published in the *Writing in Asia* series as *The Pilgrim* in 1975 and which in 1978 was honoured with the first ASEAN Literary Award for the Novel. *Drought* was first published in 1972 in Jakarta under the title *Kering.* His other novels are *Merahnya Merah* (The Redness of Red, Jakarta 1968) and *Kooong, The Story of a Pigeon* (Jakarta 1975). Iwan Simatupang died in 1970.

Iwan Simatupang is regarded as a major innovator in the field of the Indonesian novel. He challenged traditional concepts of plot and characterisation. His novels are marked by his razor-sharp sense of humour. The panel for the First ASEAN Literary Awards described *The Pilgrim* as confronting "the crisis of sensitivity, represented by the archetypal searcher, in the modern world" and as "a courageous and poignant portrayal of the human condition".

Harry Aveling (Swami Anand Haridas), the translator of both *Drought* and *The Pilgrim,* is Dean of the School of Human Communication, Murdoch University, Perth, and is a noted translator of modern Indonesian and Malay literature. Other translations by Harry Aveling in the *Writing in Asia* series are *The Fugitive* by Pramoedya Ananta Toer, *Srengenge* and *Al and Other Stories* by Shahnon Ahmad and *From Surabaya to Armageddon: Indonesian Short Stories.* Forthcoming are *Sri Sumarah and Other Stories* by Umar Kayam, *Lazy River* by A. Samad Said, *Kooong* by Iwan Simatupang and *The Prince of Mount Tahan* by Ishak Haji Muhammad.

The cover painting, "Perception" by a leading Indian artist, J. Swaminathan, is reproduced by courtesy of Pundole Art Gallery, Bombay.

Heinemann Educational Books (Asia) Ltd

41 Jalan Pemimpin, Singapore 20
Suite 4012-3, The Regent of Kuala Lumpur,
Jalan Imbi, Kuala Lumpur 06-23, Malaysia
P O Box 6086, Tsim Sha Tsui Post Office,
Kowloon, Hong Kong

LONDON EDINBURGH MELBOURNE AUCKLAND
JOHANNESBURG NAIROBI LUSAKA IBADAN
NEW DELHI KINGSTON

This book was first published by P.T. Gunung Agung in the Indonesian language under the title *Kering.*

First published 1978

Typeset by Collie's International, Singapore
Printed in the Republic of Singapore by
Chong Moh Offset Printing Pte. Ltd.

INTRODUCTION

Drought represents the most extreme expression of Iwan Simatupang's vision of the world. As he wrote in an earlier novel, *The Pilgrim (Ziarah)*: "The problem facing man is not his goodness or evil, truth or deceit, beauty or ugliness, but whether the ultimate essence of humanity will survive when he reaches the outermost reaches of his own being."[1]

The main character is an intellectual, who is too intelligent to live with the rationalised cruelty of the society around him. He views himself as a failure. To find himself, "our hero" (he has no other name) is forced to flee normal society. He gives up his studies and becomes a transmigrant, one of the thousands of Indonesians who have left the densely populated island of Java to begin life again as farmers in the sparsely-settled "outer islands". (The *average* population density of Java was 1,324 persons per square mile, in 1961.[2]) The life of the transmigrant, be he government-sponsored or self-motivated ("spontaneous"), is a hard one, requiring continuous labour in harsh unrewarding conditions. Disaster is an ever-present risk. One Indonesian periodical recently described transmigration, not as a way of improving the life of farmers, but as a scheme for "spreading poverty".[3] Our hero is prepared to struggle, but the unexpectedly long dry season — the drought — defeats him. He wants to live alone, to struggle and understand himself. Instead he is confronted with the stupidity of the doctor, who seeks to cure his "madness", and the bureaucrat, who wants to send him back into the centre of the drought again. Normal society is savage and vindictive, despite its apparent benevolence, Iwan Simatupang seems to say; it can only be fought with the wisdom of the lunatic.

1. Iwan Simatupang: *The Pilgrim* (Heinemann Educational Books (Asia): Hong Kong, 1975), p. 82.
2. A.M. Sievers: *The Mystical World of Indonesia* (Johns Hopkins University Press: Baltimore and London, 1974), p. 329.
3. "Bukan Menyebar Kemiskinan, Bukan?", *Tempo,* 13th July 1974, pp. 6-8.

Our hero has a number of assistants in his struggle against normal society. The first is his friend, the leader of an international smuggling organisation. The second is his friend's mistress, the so-called VIP, who bears our hero's child, conceived in a shameful display of public sexual intercourse. The third, and most important, is a bandit. The historian E.J. Hobsbawm has defined a bandit as, legally, "anyone belonging to a group of men who attack and rob with violence". He points out that the term applies equally to "those who snatch pay-rolls at an urban street corner" and to "organised insurgents or guerrillas who happen not to be officially recognised as such".[4] (These were common after the end of the Indonesian Revolution in 1949.) The bandit is a symbol of political freedom gone corrupt. Strangely, there is an innocence about these criminal outsiders: they have chosen the direction of their own lives deliberately, they do not follow the rules blindly, nor do they seek to hurt others in the name of a higher morality for their own benefit. They are beyond "good and evil".

Underlying the novel is Iwan Simatupang's mordant humour. He has a keen eye for human pomposity, arrogance and hypocrisy. He delights in exaggerating scenes to incredible lengths, and in the to-and-fro of outraged logic.

And yet, there is more. Ultimately *Drought* is an optimistic novel. The hero discovers that he cannot live alone, mocking others. He must turn his back on his failure, and try to do something positive, in the company of his fellow men. Whether he succeeds or not does not greatly matter, at least he will have tried. The "outermost reaches" of a person's being are found not in selfish isolation, but in the attempt to build a new and humane community.

Harry Aveling
(Swami Anand Haridas)

4. E.J. Hobsbawm: *Bandits* (Weidenfeld and Nicolson: London, 1969), p. 13.

ONE

Bone dry. The fields were now barren cracked plains.

He walked. The long shadow of his body danced at even greater length over the cracked lines. It was like an abstract painting: a strange man, his body broken into separate pieces, dancing over the broken earth.

The mid-day sun knew no pity. Its heat lashed against the sky. There was not a single drop of moisture. Here and there the trembling sky exhaled shimmering clouds close to the face of the ground.

He reached the small spring, just behind the small hill, at the northern edge of his field.

The spring was dry. It was finally dry. That it had gone on giving water as long as it had, until yesterday, seemed to him—and the other farmers around him—a miracle in itself. Other wells had dried up long ago, turned into small holes and filled with dried, flaking mud.

They had even begun to bet on it: would the well be dry in the morning? Early the next day they would run there to see if water still flowed. Those who won the bets were delighted. Those who lost—were delighted too. There was still water.

This time no one was delighted. Those who had been there earlier made no attempt to hide their grief and disappointment. Kettles, bamboo containers, cans and pots lay scattered at random around the hole.

A large wooden pole lay embedded in the eye of the well and told of their futile efforts to gouge water out. It told of their disbelief and of their despair . . .

He nodded. The nod sought to fix the stake, the scattered kettles, bamboo containers, cans and pans, the dried mud and the cracked earth which had once been fields, into one logical pattern: drought.

The drought had never been as severe as this before.

His steps led him back across the cracked plains again. His feet made small craters among the cracks. Dust puffed into the air.

The cracked lines seemed to dance inside his skull. They spun nets. The nets seemed to draw increasingly tighter around him.

He took larger steps. Walked more quickly. He had to escape . . .

The nets seemed to grow larger too. Finally they formed one giant net, from which there was no possible escape. Gathering all his strength, he began running.

Running. Running.

The small village of transmigrant farmers was thrown into confusion. Their beloved village-head was running, as though chased by the devil himself.

As soon as he reached the village he fell sprawling to the ground. There was foam around his mouth. His tongue protruded. He was unconscious.

They called the medicine-man. "You were right," he told them. "The devil was after him."

He ordered them to burn incense, and to fetch a betel leaf and a pot of water.

"Stop!" the unconscious man shouted. He stood up, fresh as a daisy. They were stunned. So was the medicine-man.

"Don't waste the water!" he snapped.

They poured the water back into the jar.

"Brothers!"

Those in the village square gathered around him. Those still at home rushed out to hear what he had to say.

"The situation is extremely serious. The last well has dried up. There is no more water."

The crowd murmured. They already knew that.

"What are we to do? What can we drink? How can we cook—assuming there is anything to cook if things go on as they are?"

He looked at the faces near him and read: fear, despair and confusion.

"We asked the authorities for food. They did not reply. From what I have heard, they ran out of food a long time ago. Why? Because of the drought. The secondary crops failed completely. Anything that did grow was thin and quickly died. There was no water for spinach. Or for papaya. Imagine spinach without water! Impossible!''

Again the crowd murmured. They knew that too.

''Well, what will we drink?''

''I think you should place the question in its full context, sir. In my opinion the problem really is: what do we eat and drink now. Or, more succinctly, how can we survive?''

The voice was authoritative, calm and very clear. It belonged to a thin dried-out man wearing glasses. Glasses, mind you. Not something one commonly finds worn by farmers. In fact a most unusual phenomenon in a developing country.

''It's true. How can we survive. We have no rice. No water. There is nothing else to eat. As far as we know, there is no way that we can get food or drink. No one will help us. That is the problem, no more and no less.''

Again he looked at the faces standing near him and read: fear, despair and confusion.

''The next problem is to decide whether we are prepared to die of hunger and thirst or not. If we are not, what can we do so that we don't?''

It was the man with the glasses again. Authoritative, calm and very clear. Suddenly everyone focused on the farmer with the appearance of a lost scholar.

He was right. That was the problem: to die, or not to die. To be or not to be.

They shivered. Frightened, desperate, confused.

''If we reject death, we must choose life. Under the circumstances, the district cannot provide for us. If we would rather live than die, our decision must be: to go somewhere else, where things are better.''

Commotion broke out. Go somewhere else? They had lived here for a long time.

The man with the glasses ignored them and left. There was further tumult as they watched him go. Each person had been coming to the same conclusion for some time. He had had no monopoly on logical thinking. The same idea had been forming in their own minds, but they could not have formulated it as clearly as he had, especially in front of the others. In any plague everyone knows the name of the disease but nobody dares say it aloud.

A short fat man ran after the man with the glasses.

"Where are you going?"

"Away. I should have gone a long time ago."

"Where?"

"To be honest: I don't know. But doubt and uncertainty are both superior to death. At the very least they mean taking a risk, a gamble. Trying again. Making an effort. And what does that mean, my friend? Living. Being alive again!"

The man in glasses was silent. His eyes shone brightly behind the glare of the afternoon sun on his glasses and he stared sharply into his friend's eyes. The little fat man swallowed his saliva.

"When are you leaving?"

"A man leaves the moment he decides to go."

"Right now?"

Glasses smiled and nodded his head.

"But it's late. Why don't you leave in the morning?"

"It doesn't matter when you leave if you don't know where you're going."

He packed his clothes and a few other necessary items neatly and efficiently into a small rattan suitcase and stood with the bag in his hand.

"You can have everything else, including the hut. What you do with them is up to you. Don't do anything if you don't want to. Throw it all away. Or give it to someone else. Goodbye."

"Aren't you going to ask me if I want to come?"

Glasses smiled and shook his head.

"Certainly not! Nor do I intend to ask what your future plans are. That is entirely your own affair. Just as my going and my future concern nobody but myself."

The little fat man swallowed his spittle once more. It was improper to betray emotion in such an environment.

"Say goodbye to the others for me."

They had reached the end of the rice-fields.

"There's no need to come any further."

They shook hands.

For a brief moment they stood motionless on the bank of the field. Their bodies seemed rooted, pointing accusingly at the drought-stricken sky. There seemed no end to the drought this time . . .

Glasses leapt over the wall. His feet made little clouds of dust as they stabbed into the barren cracked ground.

Dazedly the little fat man watched him go. Finally the bespectacled body, broken into pieces by the corrugations in the soil, vanished into the distance. Swallowed by the hot empty afternoon.

The meeting had reached a dead end. The decision was obvious. Go. Find another district to live in, eat and drink. If there was no such place, then they had no choice. They would have to ask the government, specifically the Department of Transmigration, to send them back to the villages they had originally come from.

Would those villages be able to take them back again?

They didn't know. But it was better to be hungry, even starve to death, in one's own village. They could not explain why that should be so. It was obvious that one was equally dead, whether one died during a drought in a transmigrant village or at home.

Not everyone wanted to go home.

"I'd feel too ashamed!" snapped one well-built, cruel-looking man.

"Why?" our hero snapped back at him.

"Why? Because when I left, everyone thought I had gone forever. I sold all I had. Or gave it to my kinsfolk. They had a big feast to send me off. How could I go back, like this, with nothing? I haven't earned a thing, except poverty and disgrace. I'd rather kill myself than listen to their mockery."

"Right. Right. Absolutely right. I know exactly what you mean."

The speaker was a middle-aged *haji*, one who had fulfilled the Muslim injunction to make the pilgrimage to Mecca.

Most people felt the same way. What would happen?

Our hero began to be angry. He was tired as well. And thirsty. It was too hot. The heat of the drought danced its fingers around his neck.

"I refuse to go home!"

"So do we!"

"What should we do then?"

"Anything, as long as we don't have to go back to our villages."

Our hero was disappointed. He began to realise that he had not convinced them. There was nothing left to tell them. The government had helped them with rice, water, anything they wanted, when it could. But now the transmigration officer just shook his head when he made his infrequent visits. His words were only cheap diplomacy to conceal the fact that he had nothing and was not prepared to do very much for them.

"No one has ever said that the life of the transmigrant is an easy one. It requires extraordinary stamina."

When they asked him about the possibility of his department helping them, he replied: "I'll see what can be done."

Nothing could be done about water.

"It's gone too far. You can't blame us if the wells and springs have dried up. You can't. And you can't blame us for the drought. If you want to blame someone, remember one thing. This is a backward nation. Very backward!"

They were startled.

"What do you mean?"

"The non-backward, advanced, rich nations can irrigate whole deserts. Look at America. Look at Israel. Even Kuwait, a small Arab Kingdom, but fabulously wealthy because of its oil."

"Isn't our country rich?"

"Look around yourself for the answer. If we weren't so backward, we would have bought and installed machines which could convert salt water into fresh, a long time ago."

"We shall let the state and its leaders solve that problem. You are responsible for our being here. Can you, as an officer of the Department of Transmigration, tell us what we should do next? Where should we go?"

The officer was overwhelmed.

"My dear friends. Please don't ask me to speak badly of the government I serve. As a paid employee of the state, I can only assure you that the government has no wish that any of its projects should be left incomplete, let alone collapse entirely. But, under the circumstances, the government can do no more than it has already done. The severity of the drought has upset all my department's plans. Which means in turn: the budget. In any backward nation, problems in budgeting are always solved the same way: sorry, no money. That is why all our projects fail. The advanced nations are continually advancing, the backward nations fall further and further behind. To get back to the original problem: I am not authorised to give you any advice at all. Anything I could say to keep you here, would be like casting you into even deeper hell. If I were to tell you to go, I would be destroying the project myself. The government doesn't pay me to do that. I'm sorry, I think I should return the problem to you. Do whatever seems best. Best for the country. Best for us all."

He saluted them and left.

So they would go. But not back to the various villages which had farewelled them with prayers and feasts.

The person who went to Mecca was expected to bring back a turban, holy water from the sacred well, prayer beads from Medina, and the demeanour of a genuine *haji*. How could they go home and tell everyone that the government had failed them?

No!

They had to go somewhere else!

That was what they had decided. They went back to their huts. The news of Glasses' departure inspired some of them to leave at once, even though it was night-time.

They took only the things they really needed, leaving behind them their mattresses and larger furniture. One never knew, they might be back in a few days.

Others left the next morning. The next day. And so on. Finally only our hero remained.

The departure of the little fat man left him all alone in the village.

"Are you sure you want to stay?"

Our hero smiled.

"A captain always goes down with the sinking ship."

"Do you think such heroics will serve any purpose? What are you trying to prove, if anything?"

"You've said I'm trying to prove something. That's enough, isn't it? Don't confuse things by trying to define what they are. Honour the principle, even if it has no name. No definition. Just as I honour your decision to go."

"I'm sorry if I offended you. I didn't mean to."

They shook hands. He walked to the edge of the rice-fields with the fat man.

"Stay in peace."

"Go in peace."

For a long time, our hero watched him go. The clouds of dust left by his foot-prints on the cracked barren plain showed the direction he had taken.

TWO

Everyone had gone. Except him. The transmigrant village was empty. Except for the drought. Nothing else remained.

He made an inventory. How long would the drought last? There was only one large jar of water in the whole village. One bag each of rice, corn, and tapioca. Two blocks of salt. A few slices of salted fish. A packet of matches. A tin of kerosene.

This was all they could spare. They took everything else. Provisions for a journey to an unknown destination.

He wondered which hut to destroy first. For firewood. They had already stripped the hills, for firewood.

His plan: first Glasses' hut. It was the smallest, the most rotted and the mustiest. Then the little fat man's hut. Then the rest.

He wondered how far he could stretch his supplies. If he was very thrifty indeed, he could survive three or four months. After that? He would have to wait and see.

It was some relief. His survival for at least two months was guaranteed. But then he panicked again. How could he fill his time? What work was there? And why?

The silence was hellish. The heat of the sun was unbearable. The earth was a waste land. Life was elemental. His suffering would be indescribable.

What subterfuge could he find to justify his staying in the village?

The next day he found something to do. Dig a well. He would keep digging until he found water.

And if he didn't find water? That didn't matter. The work would keep his body busy and his mind from going mad. It would take a month or two. Perhaps the drought might be over by then, it might rain.

And if it didn't rain? That didn't matter. He would keep digging. If necessary right through the earth until he surfaced in Mexico. Or Texas.

After examining all the wells, he chose the deepest. It was

full of spiders. It stank.

He made a long ladder from a piece of bamboo with steps of wood. The sort of ladder one could make any time. There was plenty of dry bamboo in the village.

He began digging.

His daily programme: rise at dawn. Walk around waiting for the sun to appear. Cook the whole day's food. Breakfast. Dig until midday. Lunch. Dig until late afternoon. Rest. Wash. Walk around with the setting sun. Dinner. Sleep.

After a week he saw that his body was filling out. His muscles were hardening. Emotionally he was changing too. A new skill developed: he no longer saw everything through rose-coloured glasses. He no longer felt endless self-pity for himself. The sun was a pure white ball of light: one met it with a stout heart and a fierce coursing of the blood throughout one's whole body.

The silence did not signify an absence. It was an essentially concrete thing, to be treated on its own terms.

One day, after he had finished walking, he began shouting at the sun as it bulged its way into the east.

"Good morning!"

The sun made a friendly reply through the songs of the birds and the light reflected from the lenses of their eyes.

He shouted good morning to everything he met. To the brittle crumbling shacks. To the furniture scattered at random by the over-hasty departure of the refugees. To the old jar coloured inside by filthy moss and outside by dull grey dust. Good morning to the bald hills in the distance and to the cracked plains around the village. To the blue sky and scattered blocks of cloud. To the silence which bound the whole scene into a picture of one of the possible ways of living beneath the gutter of a sky. Good morning to everything, and if God really exists—then good morning to Him too!

"Good morning!" he shouted to the match, to the bluish flame in the hearth, to the rice, to the slice of salted fish on the coals.

"Good morning!" to the smell of cooking salted fish as it dripped oil and stimulated his appetite to enormous dimensions.

"Good morning!" to himself once he had finished his

modest meal, and to the sliver of fish caught between his left molars.

"Good morning!" to the gentle feeling of happiness he could just sense, essential capital for starting the day's digging.

From that moment on, silence was banished. The village again rustled with human voices. The monologues formed conversations, dialogues. They were "monologues" because only one voice could be heard, the other voices were not for human ears.

"Hello, torn sleeping mat. How are you? Don't you try to make me sleep in the middle of the day. I have to keep digging all day. And you, hunger! Please don't ask too much. I haven't got much food left. Have I, rice? Have I, tapioca? corn?"

Then he struck his muscles. Hard. Round, as they shone in the sun.

"Grow, all of you! Grow as much as you want. Let us see what will happen to us."

The muscles did grow. They became harder. The empty village on the dry parched plateau was inhabited by a Robinson Crusoe with the build of a Tarzan. He was not only shaped like Tarzan, he acted like him too. Tarzan—being in the jungle—spoke with orang-utans, monkeys, lions and bears, our hero spoke with concrete and abstract objects. With fire, sunset, the rainbow, hunger, fatigue, and the future which was becoming increasingly more vague.

One day he fled from the hole. For some reason he had had to cough, and he was horrified when his voice roared like a hurricane. He seemed to hear a thousand monsters from a thousand legends cough simultaneously, followed by a fierce thunderous roar.

He had never heard anything like it. There was never any sound in the hole. Work was work. No matter how hard he chattered when he rested, he was equally dumb while he worked.

Suddenly he just had to cough. His lungs and chest were in utter opposition. There was no other way to overcome the tension.

The cough exploded out. The force was terrific! A thousand monsters snarling all at the same time, in a very deep, very dark cave.

His ear drums seemed ready to burst. He waited a moment. The terrible voices spun on and on, echo after echo.

Fear gripped him. He threw out his pick and the basket he used to carry dirt. Never before had he climbed out so quickly. He ran to his hut—all the huts in the settlement were his—and threw himself down on a torn sleeping mat. Panting.

He could still hear the noise. As though it had leapt out of the hole after him and was still chasing him. He covered his ears with his hands. The voices grew louder. He shut his eyes. Now he could not only hear the monsters but see them as well.

They had large bulging eyes. Long fangs. Fingers with sharp pointed nails.

One of the monsters approached him. It had red eyes and teeth the colour of the rainbow. Its nails stretched out towards him.

He leapt up and ran. Ran as fast as he could. He did not see the dividing walls, the cracked plains, the valley, the ravine, or the bald hills. He ran, ran, ran.

The voices kept on chasing him. He reached the top of a hill. "If I must die, let it be here!" he decided. He began to feel braver. "Sooner or later I will die anyway, so why be afraid?" He threw on his brakes and stood firm.

Opening his eyes, he shouted as loudly as he could:

"Hey! Here I am! Come and get me—if you dare!"

Nobody came, of course. No monster, not even the ghost of a monster. The hill was deserted. The blue sky hung above it. The drought sky.

He laughed. Loudly.

"Ha! I frightened myself. Fear—where are you? A monster—ha! ha! ha! There are no monsters. Nor shades of monsters. Nor shades of shades. Ha! ha! ha!"

And inwardly he continued:

"There is nothing here but drought. And never ending human suffering. And the inescapable conclusion that none of this is necessary."

As he climbed back down the hill to the village, he

continued jesting with the drought.

"You almost succeeded in driving me mad. Who and what are you, drought? You bring heat and dryness. You suck the moisture from the clouds and squeeze the winds dry as they swirl confusedly from one part of the earth to another. You have driven perpetually suffering humanity from the village, and widened the road so that the traffic of their misery might pass more quickly. You have wrung the damp from the earth and the tears from their eyes, drop by drop."

He was back in the village.

"Tears indeed! I cannot cry, yet still you tempt me. I have seen and known too much. No matter how much misery you plant in my heart—damn you, I will not cry. Have you forgotten that drought has dried me out? Why don't you stop playing with me? I will not cry! Why don't you send real rain instead and end this barren aeon?"

Back he climbed down the hole. How deep was it? He didn't know. How long had he been digging? He didn't know. How much longer and how much further would he dig? He didn't know.

He climbed down the ladder. And dug. And dug. And dug.

The next day the sky was as bright as it had been the day before. The horizon danced in the distance.

Scourged, scourged, scourged.

His provisions were in a critical state. He decided to eat only twice a day. And to cut his water by half.

Again he wanted to put nature to the test. He wanted to know whether he could work harder by eating less.

After the first day he decided he could. This was obvious by the size of the heap of dirt he had dug from the hole. More than the previous day.

He was delighted. Why shouldn't mankind be able to solve all its problems through the undiscovered potentialities of the human body?

So he decided to eat once a day next week. And to work longer hours, far into the night.

He could scarcely believe it. Physically he did not suffer at all. His muscles grew even harder. Sweat poured off him all day long. He was even more delighted. His conversations with the objects around him grew even more voluble.

"Good evening, sickle moon!"

The new moon bowed in the east.

"You're late this time. According to my figures, you should have been here three days ago. Nothing should stop you coming in the drought season."

It was very late. Almost dawn. He still had not slept. He wondered whether this was just because he couldn't sleep, or because he had decided while he was working that he would not sleep, not until it was very late.

He had repressed the crazy decision and worked until the sun set. After eating—he only ate once a day, at night—he forced himself to feel tired.

His eyes stayed wider awake than they ever had. Never closed at all. It was strange but he could not sleep.

He thought of other nights he had stayed awake, drinking cup after cup of thick black coffee so that he could be a graduate.

Although he was still awake when the roosters crowed, not one letter of his books had made any impression on his mind at all.

Years passed. His friends finished and took up important positions. He, because his mind was corroded with thick black coffee, could only vaguely guess what the books were about.

After many years of involvement with books and lectures, he decided to leave them all behind him.

His professors were relieved. They were no longer to be tortured by such an extravagant use of talent and intellect. He was an outstanding student, with an exceptionally clear mind. His memory was astonishing. He had every quality a graduate should have. Why then did he never sit for his exams?

"I'm not interested in paper qualifications," he told his anguished teachers.

"What else is there?" they asked.

He simply smiled.

One day he stopped attending lectures. He went to the library instead. Every night he took a bag of books home with him. He only left his house to change them.

He asked his landlady to send his meals to his room. In fact, he went so far as to ask whether he could keep a chamber pot in his room. Because she had always thought that he was crazy, mad even, she granted his crazy request. She didn't even mind emptying the pot into the toilet, cleaning it out and bringing it back to his room.

Finally he collected all the volumes in his room and returned them to the library. Then he packed his bag and paid his rent.

"I'm off. Goodbye."

She nodded and accepted the money, having decided not to ask for any explanation. "Crazy," she thought.

He ordered the trishaw driver to stop outside The Department of Transmigration.

"Are you recruiting transmigrants or not?" he snapped at the officer. The man was looking at him strangely.

"We are," the officer replied. "But not your kind."

"What's wrong with me?"

"You look more like a scholar out to do research on transmigrants than a real transmigrant."

"I'll ignore that. I don't care what I look like; I want to be a transmigrant. Do I meet the requirements or not? As far as I know, the shape of a person's body doesn't matter."

"Transmigration is the beginning of a new life. It means a lot of hard work."

"Don't you think I can work hard?"

"But you're not a farmer."

"I can learn."

"I'm afraid you might have rather a romantic idea about what it means to be a transmigrant, especially in our country. It's not a picnic, you know. Not even a scout jamboree. There wouldn't be time to read books."

"I am not going to read books."

Eventually, after the Head of the Department himself had been called in, our hero's application was accepted. He was listed as a spontaneous migrant.

"What does that mean?" he asked.

The Head of the Department, having read his application, and knowing that he was a learned man, smiled.

"I'd rather not get into an argument about it. No doubt one

could write a long study on: A methodological analysis of spontaneously-motivated transmigration in developing nations . . ."

Our hero laughed loudly.

"That's very good. Er—have you ever studied philosophy?"

"I used to. But I gave it up."

"Why?"

"I was frightened I might learn too much about myself."

Our hero laughed again.

"What a sublime sense of humour. But let's not discuss such matters. Just tell me—briefly and simply—what I need to know to be a transmigrant."

"That's not my job. Ask over there."

The Head of the Department pointed to a room. Our hero entered it alone.

After a crash course in transmigration, he was sent to a transmigrant hostel. When they were lined up the next morning to go aboard ship, he was appointed a section leader.

As they sailed, he got to know the members of his section better. They had all been farmers. Their reasons for leaving their villages and trying their luck in some unknown place as transmigrants were almost all the same. An increase in population. A decrease in arable land. The menace of marauding bands. Underground communist activity aimed at destroying communal life.

"And what about you?" our hero asked Glasses.

"My father was a farmer."

"And you?"

"You could say that I was an intellectual descended from farmers."

"What sort of an intellectual?"

"A teacher. The ideal position for a rural intellectual."

He had studied in the Electrical Engineering branch of the Technical Faculty. Perhaps the leap into an electronic world had been too much for a farmer's son straight from school. He did not take his preliminary exams, let alone his finals. In the end he taught various science subjects at high school level.

There was a girl to whom he gave private lessons in technical drawing. One day he took her to bed. After three months her skills in drawing were still mediocre, but her stomach was beginning to enlarge.

So, one day, the former student of electrical engineering, now a science teacher, decided to go into hiding and become—a spontaneous migrant.

"Not all that spontaneous, if you ask me. But you do know that the police can come to transmigrant areas as well, don't you?"

"Let them, if they want to. If God has decided that He wants me to be a transmigrant—spontaneous or any other sort—then anyone who wants to come and find me is welcome to try. I'm not afraid anymore."

"Just like the French Foreign Legion, eh?"

They laughed. For the first time they realised how wide the meaning of 'transmigrant' was. And how difficult it is for a developing nation to successfully implement a transmigration policy. A transmigrant was like a Foreign Legionaire in Dien Bien Phu, Vietnam. Whether he won or lost, he would always be a nobody. If he died, there was no guarantee that he would be decently buried.

Our hero was happy. The sudden collapse of Glasses' ideals had given him a fierce desire for adventure, ready to face anything that happened to him. Our hero felt certain that Glasses would become a good friend.

"And you?" he asked the little fat man, who was built like a landlord.

"I was a gambler. And an embezzler. I took the firm's money. Because I owned up at once, the court went easy on me. The judge and prosecutor were delighted. They settled on two year's imprisonment straight away. I accepted the sentence at once, without thinking any more about it. Last week I was released, and now . . ."

". . . you're a spontaneous transmigrant."

"More or less."

They laughed. Our hero felt certain that the little fat man would become a good friend.

"And you, sir?" our hero asked a *haji.*

The old man did not reply. He scratched his white hair and walked to the rail of the ship.

Another man — from the same village — told them that the *haji* had taken money under false pretences.

Our hero was silent. Inwardly he thought that the *haji* could probably become his friend as well.

The next day they reached port. From now on they would travel by train, then walk five kilometers. The settlement area was still jungle.

On the gangway from the ship, Glasses and the little fat man called out to our hero.

"We've all told you about ourselves. You haven't told us a thing about yourself."

He laughed.

"Me? I'm a failure."

Then he told them his story. Exactly as it had happened.

They nodded, certain he would be a good friend.

The first days were full of activity. The usual activities endured by newly arrived transmigrants. Listening to spirited speeches, serious and half-serious advice, delivered by the officials responsible for their well-being.

Our hero and his section were sent to the district furthest inland. Jungle and scrub, nothing else. Even wild animals avoided it. There were only a few springs. The district was well beyond the hills. It was said that the springs only ran in the wet season.

"Hell. What about the dry season?"

"Under normal conditions, you can still get water from the springs near the coast."

"What if things aren't normal?"

"God help us all."

"How bad is the next dry spell likely to be?"

The officer felt uncomfortable. He wiped at the sweat around his neck. It was time to go.

The three friends would not let him go.

"How bad is the next dry spell likely to be?"

"You were told repeatedly, long before we brought you here, that it takes a lot of stamina to be a transmigrant. Maybe this year's drought, or the next, will be severe. Abnormal. But there is nothing that we can do about such an eventuality. There is no answer to your question. All I can say is that if drought does come, we must face it courageously. We must do whatever is possible. The rest is up to God."

He then left quickly.

They began working. Clearing the scrub. Burning the long grass. Digging out the roots and stumps. Making small pools to catch the water. Making pipes to carry the water to underground storage tanks. Channelling some of the water to nearby fields. The fields were to be wet rice-fields.

"I think we should stick to dry rice-fields. You can't conjure wet rice-fields out of bare land without becoming over-dependent on an already inadequate water supply, which could stop at any time."

"Shouldn't we make the best possible use of the water available to us?"

"Yes. But let's be reasonable too. Turning scrubland into wet rice-fields requires a revolution. It takes enormous effort to plough and cultivate land like that. I support revolution as long as it does not end with all of us in hell. The hell of parched earth, covered with stringy grass because there is no water to grow anything else."

The speaker belonged to a different section. He had once attended an agricultural high school for a while. Now, because he was unemployed, he was a transmigrant. A spontaneous transmigrant? He didn't know.

"What's wrong with at least trying? Who knows, maybe things won't work out like that at all. The fields will survive. The springs might keep running."

Glasses was angry. He did not like half-baked lectures. The boy was not in possession of the full facts. He hadn't stayed at school long enough. Not that he himself knew all about agriculture, yet.

"You sound like a school-master, sir! I do believe in revolution and the creation of new traditions. I have no objection to turning scrubland into wet ricefields. But you mustn't forget that the fields have to survive more than just one season. We shouldn't experiment while the future is so uncertain."

The debate grew fiercer and fiercer. Eventually the three

friends carried the day. They decided to continue creating wet ricefields. Transmigration meant experimentation and risk, they told themselves. Everything else was a gamble, and depended on the existence of God. If He did exist, He would want the transmigrants to be successful. They continued planting wet rice.

The fields had already become an obsession. They thought of nothing else. Already they could see a prosperous, fertile, shady transmigrant settlement, with houses painted in various colours and healthy, well-fed inhabitants.

Their eloquence convinced the transmigration officials. Members of other sections were forced to agree, whether they wanted to or not. Except for the former student of agriculture, who asked to be transferred to another settlement.

He wrote a letter protesting to the Minister of Transmigration and sent copies to the newspapers. If the scheme was to succeed, he said, immediate steps ought to be taken to avoid recruiting vagabonds with no special skills, in particular confused scholars, amateur philosophers and addicts of American westerns about Mike Applepie and Davy Crockett.

THREE

The sky was still red-hot. The drought knew no mercy. The whole world was dry. Brittle in the extreme.

Things fell apart to the touch. Clods of earth turned to dust at the slightest breeze. A few trees stood naked, stiff like the ribs of a coffin, pointing accusingly at the sky.

The drought gave everything a special sheen. The sheen created strange, dream-like shapes.

Our hero lived in the middle of this sudden hell. Alone. Hell is the absence of other people. God's hell, the hell He promised sinners, could not be as lonely as the village was.

In God's kingdom, half of mankind would meet again, among the soaring flames and the burning ashes. The crackle of the flames would be broken by the thunderous cries of pain. And there would also be the voices of the angels.

"Hey Fatso! Get back in the middle! Keep away from the edge. You're not trying to run away, are you? Take that, and that! Ha, ha, ha!"

Fire is crucial to daily life in hell, loneliness was crucial to his daily existence in the transmigrant village. He decided to accept it, no matter what form it took.

His acceptance was absolute. Totally unconditional. In the end it became a fundamental part of his life.

Man has gone a long way towards harnessing sunlight for his own purposes. No doubt he will work out what to do with hell-fire.

Our hero ultimately conquered loneliness. First he befriended it. Then he divided it. He needed the first half to protect him against the second half.

From then on, loneliness followed him everywhere he went. He talked to it. Slept with it. Ate with it. Dug the well with it. Dreamt about it.

They did everything together. Loneliness was the constant companion of his loneliest hours . . .

Their conversations grew livelier day by day. The monologues formed dialogues. And were, therefore, no longer monologues.

In the same way that the man in hell accepts fire as an essential part of his being, our hero accepted loneliness. Whether he wanted to or not.

The "or not" meant he could do nothing else; for his own peace of mind, he had to want to accept it. Actively accept it.

He submitted to the consequences of his deliberate choice. The "desire to be alone" grew within him. Every decision — from the smallest matter involving the next few days, or the largest, involving his whole future — began from this premise. And from that moment on, that was how he wanted it to be.

The decision meant he could revenge himself on his previous life. His life prior to all this.

In his past life he had had to accept everything that happened, like it or not. Everything he had wanted — including everything he did not want — sprang from the need to live as best he could.

Never before had he had any choice.

His previous life began in his mother's womb. That was not the place to debate free-will. His father's sperm met his mother's egg and he was created. He became present by necessity and coincidence and God only knew what else.

Nor did the doctor's gown and forceps give him a chance to wonder, as they wrenched him earthwards, whether he wanted to live or not.

He was immediately involved in the routine links of the chain of life. Eat, drink, open his bowels, urinate, minor disease, serious disease, wasting disease, almost dead, get well again, have intercourse at an early age with a woman many years older than himself—all this was instinctual. Custom demanded it. Habit and legal regulation. Virtue and decency. Religion and morality. The already-existing culture patterns.

His decision to transmigrate, after leaving college, was a routine decision.

He did not choose to be a transmigrant. He became a transmigrant. It was a sudden, overwhelming impulse. If the impulse had insisted, for example, that he become an astronaut, he would not now have been in the deserted, barren transmigrant settlement but at Cape Kennedy.

The routine structure of his life had so far been entirely moulded by the natural instincts and wild fantasies which took possession of him from time to time. Instinct determined the flow of his life from below, fantasy determined it from above.

The older he grew, the more directionless the flow of the currents became. Sometimes they even conflicted, creating enormous waves and strong winds.

He liked the storms. He began to need them. Stronger. Fiercer. A day without a storm meant the most agonising emptiness.

His rebellion against emptiness brought new storms. Everything was ordained. He had only to accept it. Make the most of it.

The decision to be a transmigrant arose from such a storm. So did every other decision in his previous existence. He became a law student. Then transferred to economics. And to the History Department of the Faculty of Arts.

Then he became a soldier. After the revolution, when things were "normal" again, he became an officer in the regular army.

The normality seemed abnormal. So he went back to the hills. He joined a rebel band.

During a clash with the regular government forces, he was wounded. And taken prisoner. Coincidentally, the judge and prosecutor had served under him, as irregulars.

So he was not sentenced to death. His sentence was relatively light.

After he was released, the judge and prosecutor fought to get him a scholarship. He returned to his studies in history.

But how irritated he was at the lectures delivered by pale-faced scholars who seldom saw the light of the sun! He acknowledged the high academic worth of what they said. But they were so isolated from life and passion. From any lines which might intersect with his own life.

So he began asking questions. As time passed, more and more questions. Harder questions. His professors were at their wits' end. They felt threatened. They began to consider him a nuisance and a trouble-maker.

Under the "liberal system" of education, they could do nothing; it was up to him to decide when he wanted to be examined. The only problems he caused were intellectual. Not administrative. He was never rude to a member of the teaching staff, to an administrator or to a fellow student. On the contrary, everyone liked and admired him as a person.

His actions towards his teachers were always covered in a layer of polite language. Academic language. He was never vulgar. He never spoke merely for the sake of speaking.

They felt that he was stalking them. Deliberately. He even carried large tomes into the lecture theatre, just to quote a few pages in support of his own arguments. His rebellion was based on books and footnotes. Rebellion for the sake of nothing else but the books!

Often, when he entered with his heavy volumes, the professors cursed him and refused to proceed with their lectures.

This infuriated him.

"What sort of a professor are you?" he would shout.

Without being asked to, or ordered, he would walk to the rostrum and — give the lecture. At first his fellow students laughed. They thought he was fooling about. But after listening a little while, they began to be interested.

After five minutes, they were no longer interested. They were fascinated. They had even begun taking notes, just as they would have done had the professor been there.

The Senate was quickly convened. Our hero's lectures had been drawn to the attention of the most senior members of staff. Several professors protested. They insisted that he be declared an intellectual masturbator. Then quickly expelled from the Faculty. And from the University.

"On what grounds? Let us not forget that he only does what he does because certain professors are never available to give their classes."

The Dean was not pro our hero. But neither did he appreciate his colleagues sulking and refusing to teach.

"No respect for academic propriety!" shouted the Sub-Dean.

The Sub-Dean supported those who hated our hero. He hated every vexatious student. He hated every act of vexation and disobedience. He hated every student who became a student just to annoy and create trouble.

"Learned gentlemen! I appeal to you to be reasonable. Let us not be emotional or irrational about this. Otherwise we will be led into demagogy, as our Sub-Dean was with his reference to 'academic propriety'. May I ask exactly how the student under discussion has offended academic propriety?"

None of the professors could answer. The Dean was furious. He too was a Professor. Of History. With a special interest in the philosophy of history. He continued:

"This is no ordinary student.

"In the first place, he is older than the others. He first enrolled before the second world war began. A number of professors here were his classmates. Some even came after him. In the second place, his life has been far more variegated than that of any other student. He fought in the Revolution. He was a hero and won the Guerrilla Medal, as well as a number of other tributes to his valour. Then, because the Revolution warped him, he joined a rebel troop. He was caught and sentenced to death. Before he could face the firing squad, his sentence was revoked. Instead he was imprisoned. After his release, he was flung back into our faculty to resume his studies. In history. In the third place, he is brilliant. An excellent thinker. One of our colleagues in psychology once told me that he had seldom met anyone with such a high IQ. That, gentlemen, is the sort of person we are dealing with. Combine those three aspects into one phenomenon — how can we judge his peculiar goings on simply by labelling him: a madman and an intellectual masturbator?"

The professors were silent. The Dean continued his analysis:

"Let us calmly examine what some of you describe as 'underground lectures'. This folder contains a large number of sworn statements, made by students, that his lectures are more interesting, more refreshing and more creative than your own. They also request that he be allowed to continue giving his lectures, as long as they relate to the course."

"I protest!" interrupted the professor concerned.

It was the sulky, persistently absent, Professor of National History. His face was scarlet. He frothed at the corners of his mouth. He was breathing heavily.

"That's too much!" shouted the Sub-Dean, Professor of Comparative History.

"Absurd!" snapped the Professor of Classical History.

The Dean tried to restore order.

"I was only telling you what the students think. We don't have to agree with them."

"Thank God for that. If we did . . ." mocked the Professor of Cultural History. He caught the eye of the Sub-Dean and his allies.

"Because this special meeting has been called to deal with this difficult student, I hope we can arrive at some decision as to what is to be done."

The Professor of the History of Philosophy, with special reference to the History of Logic, asked if he might be allowed to speak.

"To give our discussion some discipline, I suggest that we restrict ourselves to the legal aspects. For example, I would like to ask, which byelaws can he be clearly shown to have broken? If he has legally infringed a regulation, we should get rid of him. If he has not legally infringed any law, we shouldn't. It's as simple as that."

"That isn't legalism, it's formalism."

The Professor of the History of Logic was shocked at the junior Lecturer in the Psychology of History's remark. But he quickly controlled himself. "Ah!" he thought, "those psychologists really do pretend to have a monopoly on the truth. They have their own jargon. And they even have their own pseudo-philosophy. There is no point in my arguing with him. They are all the same, whether they be Freudians or Jungians . . ."

"What's in a name? An attribute? Call it legalism, or formalism, or anything else you like. But I think the suggestion is sound. First we have to find out whether he has broken any regulation or not. If he has, expel him. If he hasn't, don't expel him. We can't do anything until we establish that."

The Professor of the History of Logic was delighted at the

sudden, unexpected assistance of the Professor of Cultural History. The Professor of the History of Psychology nodded deeply, as though thinking.

The Dean was delighted.

"I agree. The Sub-Dean, as the authority most conversant with the rules and conventions of our faculty, should be able to give us an answer. Has he, or has he not, infringed any of the regulations of our faculty in particular, or of the university in general?"

"Who said that I approve of either the formalistic or the legalistic approach?" snapped the Sub-Dean.

The learned assembly was at a dead end. Not that such men are ever without an argument for long.

"I am deeply concerned at the way that the Dean has handled this whole affair. He has turned a miscreant into a glamorous rebel. From the three components of his psychology, I can only conclude that we are dealing with a modern version of Robin Hood, Captain Blood, or Cyrano de Bergerac . . ."

". . . or d'Artagnan!" joked the Lecturer in the History of French Literature, with a sly wink at the Sub-Dean.

"Yes, or even d'Artagnan!" grumbled the Sub-Dean, annoyed at the joke. Inwardly he cursed Alexandre Dumas.

"The University is not a benevolent psychiatric ward. Without discipline and law, the struggle to make this university a centre of culture, founded on the endeavours of scholarly and virtuous men, will be of absolutely no avail. Not that I wish to close my eyes to the differences between our students. It would be wrong to consider them all the same. But any special favour shown a student whose range of experience is as broad as this student's is, must not be allowed to throw the administration of the university into chaos. A confused administration is the beginning of anarchy. And who knows what awaits the university once anarchy takes hold of it?"

The Sub-Dean watched the effect of his words on his colleagues with delight. The Dean said nothing. He knew the direction the Sub-Dean was moving in. "Very shrewd," he thought to himself.

"It is true. The byelaws of the University in general, and of our Faculty in particular, do not, could not possibly, formulate the offence committed by this student. But let me ask just one thing: Are there no other offences than those written down in the lawbooks? Nevertheless, prosecutors continue to press for certain sentences. And judges do make their own decisions."

"I protest. We are neither prosecutors nor judges."

"I protest too!"

"Hell!" thought the Dean. He had once been the chairman of a regional nationalist committee at the beginning of the Revolution. The political bigwigs and military warlords had never been as noisy as this lot. There were the same taut necks. The only real difference was that the faculty used foreign terminology more often. And they nearly all wore glasses, had high foreheads, little or usually no hair, and spoke with assumed modesty in sentences which were far too long.

"I didn't say you were. Answer me one thing. What ought we to do, if — because of this reincarnation of Robin Hood, Captain Blood or Cyrano de Bergerac . . . oh yes, or d'Artagnan — certain professors refuse to meet their obligations? In other words, resign?"

The meeting was thrown into uproar. Yet again.

"That is rather oversimplifying the problem," the Sub-Dean remarked wearily.

The Dean was close to apoplexy.

"Do I take it that you are thinking of resigning as well?"

There was further uproar. The Sub-Dean was trapped. What should he say? Should he live or die? he wondered to himself.

"Yes. I resign. Precisely."

The Dean was relieved. His breathing returned to its normal measured calm.

"Good. I accept your resignation. With immediate effect."

Further confusion. The Dean quietened them down.

"Fortunately the final decision is not for me to make. It is for my superiors. The Vice-Chancellor, his Registrars, the Academic Council. And last of all, of course: the Minister of Culture and Education."

The Sub-Dean, no longer considering himself Sub-Dean, stood and packed his brief-case.

"Gentlemen: I see no point in my remaining any longer. I do resign. You will receive my written confirmation this afternoon. I wish you well. Thank you for the cooperation you have given me during my term of office.''

Suddenly one of the office staff entered and handed the Dean a piece of paper. He read it, then leapt to his feet and chased the former Sub-Dean, who was now at the door.

''Sir! Wait a moment, please!''

''I see no point in waiting. I've resigned, do you hear me?''

''Sit down, please. This letter might change your mind.''

They both sat down. The Dean then leapt to his feet again.

''The letter cancels out the whole difficult debate. It comes from the student under discussion. Please allow me to read it.

Honoured members of the Senate. For the sake of my own sanity, I hereby resign from the Faculty I love so much. Regretfully I have come to the conclusion that the University can give me no more than it already has. Please accept my profound apologies for the trouble I have unwittingly caused you all. Yours faithfully. PS.: Of all the lectures, I most enjoyed those in comparative history.''

The meeting was silent. The Dean's face was red. His voice cracked. Quickly he took out his handkerchief and pretended to clean his glasses.

The former Sub-Dean, the Professor of Comparative History, sat stunned in his chair. He tapped on the green felt cloth of the council table to indicate that the meeting was over.

There was a long silence. Finally the Professor of Cultural History said:

''So in the end he really was a modern Robin Hood, Captain Blood, Cyrano de Bergerac, or d'Artagnan. A tragic hero. A heroic tragedian. He has once more shown us how we ought to deal with difficult problems. Let us honour him a moment. Perhaps in the future our lectures will have new dimensions because of him, no matter what it is that we teach. The problem is solved. I hope the Sub-Dean will accept his former position once again.''

The members of the faculty mumbled their approval, then dispersed.

When all the other faculty had gone, the Dean remained in his chair. He was re-examining the significance of tragedy in the development of historiography. What was history if not tragedy?

"Hm, the whole issue arises once more, just because a student leaves . . ."

He stood. Packed his bag. And left.

FOUR

The day finally arrived when there was no food. From three to two to one and now no meals a day. How much further could he fight nature?

"All right, what else can I do?" he asked himself; these days he spoke more to himself than to anything else.

Precisely. Whether he wanted to or not, he had to eat nil times a day. He was forced to live as he did, for as long as he could. Nothing and no way could be more extreme than that nought.

So he began digging. Digging. Digging.

The further down he dug, the higher the heap of dirt at the edge of the hole became. Always. The deeper the valley, the steeper its walls.

He was amazed. Was that what they called logic? Then why wasn't it: the harder he worked, the more he needed to eat?

He stopped digging. "Eat!" he thought. How long had it been since he last ate?

Perhaps he had better just keep digging. If things had to be like this, every slight action that he was still capable of represented an example of what he could and should do. The minimal acts represented all his ideals, his desire for truth, goodness, beauty, his longing for love and need for some supreme power which was holy and merciful, his craving for drink, food and rest.

So when he used his remnant energies, it was as if he were summoning up all the other things as well. In other words, the more he dug, the more he ate . . .

He was delighted. He had been becoming increasingly anxious. The paradigm stopped that. Anxious about food. Now there was no need to worry about the future.

"You are welcome, hunger! One day I will dig right through this tiny earth. To where? Texas? No. I don't like the smell of oil. To California? No. Too much nylon and neon. Too much self-indulgence and too many newly rich millionaires, like Frank Sinatra and Sammy Davis Jr. Mexico, perhaps?"

"Yes, Mexico. If possible, a plain of peyote cactus, full of mescaline and dithyliamid lyserg, in short LSD."

Ah, LSD! The modern vitamin for modern man wanting to meet modern God, on the beatnik and hippy campuses, the Christian atheist campuses and those dedicated to the world council of churches, the restless and bored kingdoms of those who worshipped the Modern Jazz Quartet, the Beatles, Bob Dylan, Joan Baez, Zen Buddhism, Cassius Clay, Stokeley Carmichael, adored the Viet Cong, Che Guevara and all revolutionary doctrines and peoples' wars of liberation, made cults of "metaphysical murderers" such as Lee Harvey Oswald and Sirhan Bishara Sirhan, and were devoted to the films of Ingmar Bergman, Truffaut and Satyajit Ray.

Yes, Mexico, where the people wore sombreros and mantillas, grew thick moustaches and played large guitars, sang like barking dogs, about the moon, blood and desire, about poetry, lust and girls dancing flamenco, about the thunderous roar of the bullring as El Cordobes fought the fierce bull, about sorrow and doubt as the chapel bells told of the approach of Easter, about *via dolorosa* and —*ole*!

A desert in Mexico? That would be hot and dry again, just like the village. Simply, from one hell to another.

Perhaps that was all life was, a journeying between hells. Today mankind is competing to enter outer space. Everyone wants to travel to other planets. Everyone wants to leave the world bequeathed them by Adam and Noah, as quickly as they can.

There is no guarantee that any other planet is better than this one. Who knows, perhaps the other planets are the hell God promised us in his various holy books.

Suddenly he was shocked by a yellowing which seemed to stretch right across the sky of his skull. Things turned to yellow before his very eyes. The yellow world was covered with yellow balls, one of which was yellower than the rest. They flew about in the air. Then they broke, one after the other. New balls formed, yellower than the others. Finally, and very slowly, traces of purple began to infiltrate the yellow scene. The world turned green, blue, red, brown and grey.

He was fascinated. Hunger was beautiful. Had the

psychologists ever studied the colour frequencies associated with hunger?

Step by step, he scaled the ladder. What time was it? He laughed. There was only darkness and silence beneath the earth's surface. Time did not exist. Calculations made underground ignored measurement. Heavy or light were meaningless, everything that fell fell to earth.

On the surface, it was late at night. It was dark, there were no stars. No stars meant night and fog. And fog meant moisture and, eventually, rain.

Rain? He laughed. Could he still remember what rain was like? What was 'wet'? Or 'cold? He floundered, unable to remember. Rain was ancient history. He felt the same about rain as he had done about a picture of the pyramids, a statue of the Buddha, or the sign of the cross . . . None of them meant anything to him. He lived in an age when astronauts walked on the moon and other planets, and spelaeonauts dived down to the centre of the earth, as he did — one of the first unnoticed and unpublicised pioneers.

He walked to the water jar. Or, more precisely, he meant to walk to the water jar. But it was so dark that he accidentally stumbled against it and broke it . . . The pot shattered. The cold water flowed over his toes . . .

"It's smashed!" he shouted hoarsely, broken-heartedly.

Finished. His food was gone. So was his drink.

He was tired. Very tired. It was very late at night. Pitch black.

There were no stars.

"It's broken! There's nothing left!" he shouted as he ran out of the hut.

Or, rather: he meant to run out of the hut. The starless night was merciless. Night held his kicking and flailing body on both sides.

The walls and pillars of the hut flew left and right. He fell back to the ground.

"Finished! Broken!" he screamed.

He took his last match and burnt the half-destroyed hut.

He ran to the ricefields. Rather: he meant to run to the ricefields.

The starless night smashed his head against a tree. A naked, broken tree, pointed at the sky.

He rolled on the ground.

When he woke, he could smell disinfectant on the white sheets and pillow slip. He thought back to the starless night — without knowing how long ago that was — and mentally solved a problem.

There could be no doubt. He was somewhere else. The sparkling whiteness and the smell of disinfectant could only mean he was in a hospital.

"That's correct. You are in a hospital."

"How did you know what I was thinking, doctor?"

The bespectacled, bald doctor smiled.

"How did you know I was a doctor?"

Our hero mumbled an oath. "Damn!" he thought. "I thought I was finished with people like him."

"What are your plans for me?"

"Our plans are limited to getting you well again. And that depends on you. You can only get well if you want to get well. When you want to leave, I will know that you're cured."

"Hm," thought our hero. "He must be a psychiatrist. I'm in a mental institution."

"Before we discuss whether you have any right to cure me or not, allow me to ask a few trivial questions."

"Such as?"

"How did I get here? And when?"

The doctor left the room for a moment. Then he returned with the transmigration officer.

"Oh, I see. You can go now."

The transmigration officer was shocked. His anger rose.

"Wait a minute!" he snapped. "I'm not a nurse. You can't throw me out like a stray dog."

"There is no need to wait. You are not a nurse. You are not a stray dog. I'm asking you as politely as I can: Get out! I can't bear to look at you."

"Disgusting!"

"The choice is yours. You can stay, and I will go. Or you can go, and I will stay."

The doctor quickly whispered something to the officer and the latter left. At the door he turned and shouted:

"Disgusting!"

The doctor and our hero looked at each other. The doctor tried to smile. He failed.

"So if I understand things correctly; the transmigration officer finally returned to the settlement . . ."

"The whole settlement had been burned down," the doctor added.

"Burned down?"

"Obliterated. Completely destroyed. Nothing left but the scorched ground. The transmigration officers found you right at the edge of the black. You were unconscious."

"Oh. What were they doing there?"

"Routine inspection."

Our hero laughed.

"Fire inspection?"

After his laugh died away he continued:

"And the only result of their inspection was my removal to a lunatic asylum."

He laughed again. Loudly. Ferociously.

"Why wasn't I taken to a general hospital before being brought here?"

"This is a general hospital. This part is the psychiatric ward."

"So you're the head doctor?"

The doctor sniggered. Our hero laughed more loudly.

"There's no need to be rude. When you're well, you can spare me your insults by leaving the ward."

"I'm sorry, I didn't mean to be rude. But I do want to get out as soon as I can — out of this ward and out of the hospital as well. Otherwise you might simply transfer me to another ward. No doubt you are all convinced that I am sick. Perhaps you might even be tempted to send me to obstetrics . . ."

He laughed again. Loudly. Ferociously.

The doctor raised his eyebrows. He tried to laugh and couldn't. Instead he left in a hurry. Soon he returned, with another doctor. An older man. With white hair. And glasses with very thick lenses.

The older man advanced, smiling like Einstein. Before he had a chance to open his lips any wider, our hero pounced.

"You're a psychiatrist, aren't you? A professor of psychiatry? He's after a second opinion, isn't he? Don't waste your time, effort or thinking on me: I am not sick!"

He stood, saluted them both and walked out the door.

The gatekeeper stopped him. His clothes belonged to the hospital. "State property!" the gatekeeper shouted.

"Then give me something else!" our hero snapped.

He had come with nothing. His underpants were dirty and charred. The hospital superintendent gave him a cheap pair of cotton pyjamas.

"Although these are state property too, I have much pleasure in presenting them to you," said the superintendent, as though he were giving away an atomic reactor.

"What a joke!" thought our hero as he looked at the striped pyjamas with amusement. "Still it's better than being naked." The pyjamas were very large. "I look like a clown in a circus!" he decided, laughing.

Outside the gate he was met by the transmigration officer.

"You're everywhere, it seems," he said, half-amused, half-resentful.

Then he climbed into the Land-Rover and sat next to the officer.

"I can understand why you hate me. You're angry because of the power I had over your life."

"That's one of your duties too, isn't it — understanding. Well what happens once you understand something?"

The officer smiled. An official smile.

Our hero was annoyed.

"Where are you taking me?"

"You'll see."

"Stop!"

"What's wrong?"

"I'm old enough to know where you're taking me. If you won't tell me, I won't come."

"Where would you like to go?"

"Where the hell am I?"

He scrambled out of the jeep. It slowly followed behind him.

"All right, I'll tell you. I want to take you back to the office."

"What for?"

"My superior wants to talk to you."

"About what?"

"I don't know. I think he's considering sending you back again."

Our hero stopped. His eyes bulged.

"Back? Back where?"

"Where you came from, of course."

His anger suddenly vanished. He laughed. Loudly. Passers-by were amazed at the sight. A man, wearing striped pyjamas and laughing as he walked, followed slowly by a Land-Rover.

"Now you listen to me. I have never owned a thing. So I don't come from anywhere. I'm not the sort of person that ever goes back. I go forward. My ticket has no return portion on it."

They were close to the ministry. He shook the officer's hand.

"I'm sorry. I've made life hard for you. For a lot of people. I didn't mean to. But I can't speak without offending someone or other. Words are too autonomous these days. We have no control over them. We speak. The words take on a separate existence. They become equal to ourselves. Sometimes greater. They control us. The tragedy is that we are under the power of so many different words. All the words we could say at the one time. They could all rule us if they wanted to. And because they would want so many different things, we could never satisfy them all. In the end, we would try to fulfil what we thought was the common will, the average expectation, of all of them. Not the exact wish of any of them, but simply what we assume them all to want. In other words: we never hit the precise meaning of any word we use, we are always a little to one side. There is a gap in everything we say. In every sentence. It is the same gap which we find in human relationships. And in every human action. There is never an exact correspondence."

He shook his hand again.

"Stay in peace. I'd rather you stayed in peace than that you went in peace. Give my respects to your superior. He's a good man, I suspect. Thank him for his goodwill towards me. And apologise for me. I failed him. Failed you all. I am a migrant, not a transmigrant."

He let the officer's hand fall.

"Stay in peace."

His light steps led him into a lane. The lane was too narrow for the jeep.

He left the other end of the lane, once he had made certain that the officer was not following him. Not the officer, nor anyone else. He had to be somewhere else.

But where? He was excited every time he asked that. Stimulated to go: forwards. Where or how were secondary problems. Not immediately relevant. The fundamental thing was: keep going.

How and where would always turn up along the way. The street corners themselves would say: this way!

The more corners there were, the more excited he would get. So many roads going in so many different directions.

Every corner said: forwards.

He looked for a corner. Standing in the middle of the road he closed his eyes and began to walk. The road he took would be the path he followed.

It had never failed. Now he was at a crossroads. Seven roads converged.

He shut his eyes, took a deep breath and began walking.

The simultaneous blare of car-horns startled him. A large sedan stopped right in front of him, its bumper-bar kissing his knees.

"Are you trying to kill yourself?" screamed the driver, a little fat man.

"If you are, go and do it somewhere else. Don't ask me to do the job for you."

Suddenly the little fat driver screamed. He jumped out of his car. He ran and embraced our hero.

"It's you!"

"It's you!"

They embraced each other in the middle of the intersection.

In the middle of the traffic jam.

The choir of car-horns became more vulgar.

"Very moving!" shouted one driver. His face was red, wet with sweat.

"Why don't you go and make love somewhere else and leave the rest of us alone?"

"Homos!"

A row of truck drivers laughed. Some whistled. Others clapped.

A foreigner, driving a car with CD licence plates, took a lot of photos.

The little fat man quickly dragged our hero into his car. They left with a roar. After a while the traffic jam melted.

The little fat man took our hero home. His house was in a first class area. It was new, expensive, exactly right for a nouveau riche.

In fact it was not a house but a modern furniture showroom. The consequence of a flood of American magazines on home decoration, home gardening, and God only knew what else. The sort of house that displayed a great deal of luxury and very little love or beauty.

"Is it yours?" our hero asked, awed.

The little fat man nodded proudly.

"That didn't take long."

"Three months."

"I can't believe it."

"Three months. Exactly."

"How did you get rich so quickly?"

"I'm surprised you can ask such a stupid question. It takes some people less than an hour."

Our hero nodded.

"Oil?"

"The age of Rockefeller is over."

"Then how?"

"Hard work."

"What sort of a work?"

"Smuggling. Counterfeiting."

Our hero was silent. Stunned. Not by the smuggling and counterfeiting, but by the calm way his friend referred to them.

"Even that takes more than three months preparation, I would have thought."

"It does if you start from scratch. It doesn't when everything is set up and ready to go."

Then he told his story. How he left the transmigrant settlement and came to town. How Glasses approached him and asked him to be second-in-command.

"Second-in-command? What was he in command of?"

"He was the head of a smuggling and counterfeiting organisation."

"Where is he now?"

"Dead. A naval patrol shot him a week ago. He was in his speedboat. Working."

"What was he carrying?"

"Counterfeit American dollars, counterfeit pounds sterling, and gold and silver bars."

"How much was it all worth?"

"At least a million pounds sterling."

"My God! What a bonus for the sailors."

The little fat man laughed.

"If you mean a bonus of bad language, you're right. They killed him but they couldn't stop the boat."

"So the million pounds is safe?"

"Sure."

Our hero congratulated his friend, although he could not understand why the gods should choose two transmigrants to be the head of an international counterfeiting and smuggling ring.

The little fat man laughed.

"Former transmigrants or not, it doesn't really matter. We can use anyone. Former presidents, professors, murderers, drug addicts, film stars, international couriers, anyone at all. Women, transvestites, men, anyone. The applicant must be clever, courageous and resourceful. Not just clever at arithmetic and talking quickly, but also at planning top level strategy. Knowing how to approach and make friends with senior officials, especially from the navy, the taxation department, the department of immigration, the harbour commission and the police force. He or she must have an extensive knowledge of the business world. Facility in a number of local and foreign languages. An ability to mix easily with the upper class. An understanding of national, several foreign, and international systems of law. Maritime law. The law relating to the skyways. An awareness of who's who in Interpol, where they are stationed, the things they enjoy, their weaknesses, and so on."

Our hero was amazed.

"Can you do all that?"

The little fat man laughed.

"Of course not. But I can do more of it than anyone else in the organisation."

"So you're the king."

"At the moment I am. Who knows about tomorrow? In this sort of organisation one is only king until one's shot, axed or poisoned. By the state, a rival organisation, a jealous colleague, or by the inevitable Brutus one always finds in any band of thieves and pirates."

The little fat man pushed a bell on the wall. A beautiful woman appeared, dressed in a transparent lacy nightgown.

"Is this one of the other items you've acquired in the last three months?"

The little fat man laughed. The woman sat on his lap, kissed him on the mouth, and bit his left ear.

"No. I inherited her from Glasses. She prefers leaders. Her trade mark is VIP. It doesn't matter how much money a man has, she won't look at him if he isn't a real man — strong-willed, handsome, daring. She only likes rich Gatotkacha's*."

Our hero stood and bowed.

"Well it's been nice meeting you again. Especially since your work seems so congenial."

"What do you mean?" shouted the little fat man.

"I'm going."

"Going? Going where?"

"On."

The little fat man was very disappointed. Heartbroken.

* *Gatotkacha:* a character in Javanese shadow-theatre, renowned for his strength and courage.

"'Don't be too proud with that 'Onwards! Ever onwards!' of yours. I know you wouldn't ever take anything from some one else. But just look at you. You're as thin as a dry stick. A flagpole dressed in cheap cotton pyjamas. I'm not offering you charity. Please stay and rest, until you're stronger."

"Who said there's anything wrong with me?"

"Stop pretending. You'll still be saying you're well the day you die, won't you. Like the holy men fasting and abusing their bodies month after month — I'm fine, I'm fine. Spiritually they are fine. Then they die, clinically and philosophically. Look at yourself properly. You can't call that bag of bones 'fine'. What are you trying to prove by your physical suffering? Do you want to be a second Buddha? Be like the Beatles. First they worked until they were as wealthy as lords, then they turned to spiritual matters — yoga, Zen Buddhism, even pilgrimages to the Himalayas. Get cash before you get religion. Buy your Rolls Royce, then read the sacred *Veda.*"

Our hero laughed. Then, suddenly, he was serious.

"Do you want me to stay for my sake or yours?"

The little fat man lifted his eyebrows.

"Explain yourself. I don't understand you.

"All right. I know what you're like. We're friends, aren't we?"

"Yes. But so what?"

"I don't doubt that your original invitation was well meant. But with you, good motives are always succeeded by other motives. And the other motives are not usually as pure as the first ones, even if they are more urgent. Impure. Evil. They only concern yourself. They are selfish and proud."

"Why shouldn't I be proud of myself once I've done something good for someone else?"

"No reason. But anything you do for yourself always seems to get you into trouble."

"I'm used to trouble."

"I know that. You always seem to choose the most complicated trouble possible."

"Even if I do, that's my responsibility. My business and no one else's."

"No it isn't. You are only kind to people you know will help

you once you get yourself into difficulty."
"Go on."
"They become involved in your problems."
"And then?"
"And then you point your finger accusingly at them and shout: 'This is all your fault!' "
"And finally?"
"You withdraw in your elegant way and find someone else you'd like to help . . ."

The little fat man was silent. He sent the VIP back to her room.
"So you won't stay?"
Our hero laughed. He moved closer to the little fat man, his dear friend.
"There is no point in discussing that. The real question is whether I need to rest or not. Rest from what? Why? Besides I don't think I could cope with your sudden transformation: from a drought stricken transmigrant settlement to the headquarters of a gang of smugglers and counterfeiters. It's too much like a detective-story . . . Write your own dime novel if you like, but please leave me out of it. I don't want any part at all. You have my sincere sympathy."
For a moment he looked silently into his friend's face.
"Do you mind if I hope we meet again soon?"
The little fat man smiled. He shrugged his shoulders, the smile came from some distant heaven.
"Sell yourself as dearly as you can, before the state, another gang, or Brutus shoots you through the skull. Live life to the full. Then go down fighting. The king is dead! Long live the king!"
The little fat man was very moved.
"Do you mind if I ask where you're going?"
"I never know where I'm going. Not even when I'm going nowhere. There's no point in any of us asking."
The little fat man shook his head and swallowed hard several times. His face was flushed. He took out his wallet.
"At least don't refuse me this. Something for the road. Buy some other clothes too."

They both laughed loudly.

Our hero patted his friend on the shoulder. Then he ran quickly out into the road.

''May God protect him . . .

The sun was perched on the ginger back of the hills. Once the hills were completely black and the night sky, edged in white, invited the drought stars to show themselves, the little fat man pushed the bell on the wall three times.

The VIP came. Stark naked. He hugged her, then dragged her over to another room.

The VIP sighed under the rhythmic movement of his body.

FIVE

He ran quickly to another corner. A fork in the road, close to the edge of town. One road led to another city. The other was small and unpaved, and led to a tiny subdistrict capital.

He closed his eyes. His feet led him onto the unpaved road ...

He was delighted. The hardest task was over. He wondered why one had to choose all the time when the best thing was simply to live. To close one's eyes and start walking. North or South didn't matter. Paved or unpaved didn't matter. Capital city of the nation or of a tiny subdistrict didn't matter.

The gentle caress of thought cheered him. He was overjoyed. He wanted to whistle.

He whistled.

He wanted to sing.

He sang.

No one knows what he sang. Our fingers improvise on a piano, our vocal chords can improvise in our throats.

The song? Who cares? Who cares about the title, the scale, the harmony? It was a beautiful, clear night.

The stars were still shining brightly. Drought danced on the horizon. The distant dark-blue mountains were edged with a red glow. Dry lumps of mud sprawled across the ricefields.

Everything was silent. Very silent. The special silence of the dry season. The green silence of the wet season is different. It breathes freshness and fertility, the air is full of buds about to break open and flower. Because he could smell the green, he forced the buds back into the period before he began to live. The pre-life period. The cannot-live period.

A drought is different from a cemetery. The cemetery is the land of do-not-live. A dry season prolonged to a state of drought is the land of cannot-live.

Drought brings a very special sort of suffering. It is more "metaphysical". One cannot point an accusing finger at someone in the witness box and say: "This is your fault ...!"

Death, for example, can be blamed on God, or the formula $E = MC^2$, or anything else you want. Who can you blame for a drought?

Some people had tried to apportion blame for the cold war between the communist bloc and the free world, and for the subsequent underground nuclear testing. They wrote ugly pamphlets with dreary slogans about peace. But when it became clear that no one could be blamed, all sorts of reactions followed: ranging from prayers for rain to the circumcision of black cats. Those who sternly rejected the worship of idols and preached love for all living creatures were the strongest advocates of these solutions.

He was gripped by a new sensation. As he walked listlessly along the tiny listless road, among the listless fields and bald mountains, he was reminded once again of the well. He had an awareness of his relationship *to* the earth. In the well, that relationship was vertical. Now it was horizontal. He existed and therefore grew in that space between the two.

So, he decided, his present perspective was horizontal. The hills looked like hills because he saw them horizontally. The sky looked like the sky because he was looking at it horizontally.

The thought startled him. Did he see the drought as drought simply because his perspective was as it now was?

He stopped walking. Then how had he seen it before? And even before before? Before he understood the importance of horizontal vision?

What had he wrestled with in the transmigrant village, if not with drought? Why had he undertaken his major act of rebellion, digging the well, if not because of the drought?

Sitting on the edge of the dirt road, he pulled up a leaf of dry grass and began chewing it.

He decided that the drought was beginning to affect him. The angle of vision didn't matter. A drought was still a drought. Still dry, hot and listless. At best, it was the quality of a person's feelings about drought which changed. But either horizontally or vertically, one was still bound *to* the earth.

He decided the real problem was *in*. *In* and *with*. *In* and *with* what didn't matter, as long as one was *in* and *with* something.

The something could even be hell. But there had to be something, so that one was never alone.

Elated, he spat out the crushed grass. He stood and stared at the horizon.

Another problem had been solved. He would never again be lonely, he thought. Even in the loneliest of situations, we are in and with our loneliness. In and with ourselves.

He kicked a pebble and began walking. Again he wanted to whistle.

He whistled.

He wanted to sing.

He sang.

He chewed on a song which he improvised from the feeling aroused by the bright sky, the burning hills in the distance, the prolonged drought, and—in and with.

If you want to continue, drought, do so. If you want to continue, suffering, do so. If you want to stay, loneliness, do so. I am not afraid. I am not alone ...

Gradually, as he walked, he became more and more surprised. He had not met anyone or anything. He had not passed anyone or anything. "What a strange town," he thought. "What a strange road. Perhaps the people don't like to go anywhere. Perhaps they don't like visitors either."

Then how did they live? The science of Economics teaches that that sort of isolation requires self-sufficiency, autarchy.

In that case, the district must be rich. Industralisation and efficient agriculture. According to the terms—which he had once read in a dirty, torn scrap of newspaper at the edge of a road—adequate funds and forces were those which were adequately processed and adequately redistributed.

The ideal society! Utopia on earth, and therefore not utopia at all. I must get there as quickly as I can, he decided. The central village must be a model town. A pilot project.

He walked more quickly. He wanted to get there as quickly as he could. He wanted to see the clean streets. The rubbish tins along the gutters, painted in various colours. The giant flower-pots in the middle of the roads, with multicoloured flowers. And the multistoried buildings. Grand offices, filled with paintings, sculptures and mosaics. The peoples' flats, furnished in the very latest styles. The garages with the magnificent cars shaped like nuclear ballistic rockets. The washing machines: push the button, dirty shirt in here, clean ironed shirt out there. No human labour required, except wearing the shirt and making it dirty once more. On every corner there would be a fountain, with statues, pictures and flowers.

He hurried. He was no longer just walking. He was like a man in a walking race, that special sport for bored middle-class citizens with nothing better to do with their time. There are car-races, boat-races, plane-races, even snail-races and tortoise-races, so why shouldn't there be walking-races which are not running-races? In short, races in which the competitors swing their hips like frogs? The term 'race' was, perhaps, paradoxical —but what the hell? Basically: one person fired a gun, others took photos, while a whole lot of others—middle class citizens as well—watched, and chatted, ate peanuts, sucked peppermints, cheered, clapped, and jumped up and down excitedly. Basically a pleasant way to fill in an empty day. Was the pleasure genuine? What the hell? If people amused themselves for their own amusement, what the hell? They kept the photos. Bought them. Cut them out of the papers and stuck them in expensive albums. And stared at them in awe until their eyes fell out ...

Suddenly he was revolted. "I hate you!" he shouted at the middle class citizens he had created in his head.

He ran ...

Because he was revolted, he ran very quickly. So quickly that the dust rose in clouds at his heels. The bald hills seemed to be flying. Like train carriages in the distance, running in the opposite direction.

"Now let's see what happens when I add the sensation of speed to the sensations caused by a horizontal perspective," he pondered. He ran more quickly. Then he momentarily shut his eyes. "There it is," he decided. The lines met in a dark purple spot ...

He opened his eyes again.

Were the hills, running with him, hills because (1) of the horizontal perspective, or (2) he was running? How would they change if he ran at different speeds? Would the changes be gradual or fundamental? If the changes were merely a matter of gradation, how did the hills now regard themselves, and how did he regard them? If the change was fundamental, *idem ditto:* how did they regard themselves, how should he?

He felt a different sort of revulsion. "I hate you!" he shouted, at himself. "Who am I trying to impress?" he cursed. He felt like a Classical Greek marathon runner, who had suddenly had the misfortune of solving a very intricate philosophical problem in the middle of a long, lonely run around the hills.

"I think I'd better take things easier," he decided. He stopped running. The sweat was pouring off him. His pyjamas were soaking wet. He was covered in dust. His breathing was ragged. He decided to sit down and rest for a while.

Suddenly he snapped at himself again. "Sitting down!" He began walking. "Every modern crisis begins because someone sits down. There are too many people sitting down. The physiology of sitting is the source of all the conflicting doctrines. The physiology of sitting has written book after book on the apocalypse, pseudo-apocalypses, and the collapse of modern civilisation. More men must stand up. Their backbones must form a straight line with their heads and feet. The lines must point directly at the sky. At the moment standing man obeys sitting man. This is capitalism! Communism! Imperialism! Bureaucracy! To hell with every manager and managing director. To hell with every commissar, supervisor and inspector. They are sitting men. The old world is a world of sitting men. No wonder our humanity is so corrupt! We must return to our former position. Standing. Tall and straight, head planted in the blue sky."

He walked. Walked. Walked. Without stopping.

Night came. It was pitch black.

Fog? Possibly rain?

There was not a breath of wind.

Suddenly he heard someone cough.

"Who's there?"

Silence. No sound. Nothing.

"Damn," he thought. "What was that?"

He started walking again.

A cough, again ...

"Who's there?"

No sound, nothing.

"Damn," he thought. "I must have thought I heard a cough. No one is there. I heard myself thinking."

"So," he continued, "you can hear something that is not there. It has its own existence. Nothing is the same as something."

"So," he further continued—as he walked in the pitch black—"the cough was, and was not. It was and it wasn't. What was it? A cough, of course."

He was startled. He heard the cough again. It was louder and clearer. The cough was repeated. There was a volley of coughing. Sharp, harsh, whining coughing.

"It's the cough of an old man," he decided. He would not ask anything, nor would he shout. He listened carefully. He could hear something else. A man walking. Slowly, awkwardly.

The old man coughed again. A volley of short, harsh, whining coughing.

"Damn," he thought. "Imagine meeting someone tonight! It's so dark! I won't be able to see him. How will I recognise him? Should I touch him? How?"

"Hey! Who are you?"

He shouted very loudly indeed. Had the man been on the bald hills, he would still have heard the shout.

"Who's there?" a voice suddenly asked, in exactly the same tone as the cough.

Our hero was thunderstruck. He had suddenly lost a doubt. The man who wasn't there, was there. Actually existed. He was thunderstruck by the existence of the existent.

"I asked first," he replied.

"Come closer, my son. I'm old. My hearing is not so good any more."

Closer? Which way? It was too dark to know. To come closer one has to know what one is coming closer to, and where it is. Where was the old man? And how could he be sure that the old man really was an old man, old, or a man?

His anxiety returned, hard as iron, shaped by the emptiness of his travelling. He had walked a long time, without meeting anyone at all. Coming in the opposite direction, or from the direction he himself was taking. Not even the smallest creature, such as a fly or a mosquito.

And now, suddenly, there was someone. Who claimed to be very old. No one had been on the road in front of him before sunset. And the road was a straight road. Very straight. Perhaps he couldn't see as far ahead as he used to be able to? Impossible.

He decided to stay where he was.

"Who are you, sir? Where have you come from? Where are you going?"

The man approached him across the gravel.

"I have come from the place you are going to."

"What a strange answer," he thought. A half-baked sentence torn from an absurd play. How could one dare ask anything else, after receiving such a categorical answer.

He was silent. In such a psychologically complex situation, silence was best. Let the other party take the initiative and ask what they wanted to ask.

"If I can ask, my son: what do you intend doing once you get there, the place I have just left?"

He seemed to hear the old man sit down. He was breathing heavily. He could smell him and he smelt like an old man. An old human.

He sat down too. On the gravel at the edge of the road.

"I haven't decided. For the moment I just want to get there. When I arrive, I'll do whatever seems best. If doing nothing is best, I'll do nothing."

"What a strange answer," thought the old man. How could one dare ask anything else, after receiving such a categorical answer.

The old man was silent. His feelings were definitely unsettled. Better let the young man ask the questions, he decided.

He was silent.

Our hero was silent.

The night was silent.

The earth was silent.
Silent. Endlessly.

"How difficult!" they thought in unison. Neither of them had ever before taken part in such a difficult conversation. A conversation composed of zero words. Which was not at all the same as no-conversation. There was a great tension in the silence. The tension of many conflicting thoughts carefully controlled as one thought: the inexpressible.

The dialogue was far tauter and livelier than most dialogues. Its meaning existed in a world that was prior to meaning. Its logic existed prior to logic, it was prelogical. And because it existed prior to meaning—which is not at all the same as being meaningless or nonsense—its meaning could be anything anyone wanted it to be. It could mean itself or its opposite, or both. So it had more meanings. More compact meanings.

After a long time of saying nothing, they both began to feel that they were acting very oddly. They wanted to break the stalemate as quickly as possible.

"Well, I had better ask something," they both thought at the same time.

"What ...?"

Because they both spoke at the same time, they were both startled. Especially because their question had been cut short, truncated, left hanging in the clouds.

"Well, I had better keep quiet while he asks his question," they both decided.

They both keep quiet.

The common silence surprised them both. "He isn't going to ask anything after all," they both cursed. "Well, I think I had better ask my question now. He isn't saying a word ..."

"What ...?"

They were both startled again. Stunned. Again they had both begun their question at the same time and again their sentences had been left incomplete, truncated, and hanging in the clouds.

"You bastard!!" shouted our hero as loudly as he could. He was furious.

The man leapt to his feet. It was true. It was a shout, a real shout. He had not just imagined the shout, or mistaken something else. It was a shout, complete with vowels, consonants, phonemes, morphemes, and heaven only knew what else.

The old man was shocked. The sky seemed to be falling on him. He was so surprised that he could not speak a single word, a single letter. He said nothing ...

Our hero immediately regretted the effect his thunderous scream had had on the old man. He regretted his honesty. His spontaneity. His naturalness. His authenticity. He was sorry that he had been rude to an old man.

He was ashamed. So ashamed that he could not speak a single word, a single letter. He said nothing ...

The old man was silent.

Our hero was silent.

Was silence silent too?

Silent. Endlessly.

Our hero was startled. He could hear the old man crying.

"Damn," he thought. "The old man is crying. I shouldn't have called out. He thought I was shouting at him. I'm crude. Only an ignorant and uncivilised beast would shout at an old man in the dark. I'm an animal. An ape."

"You ape!" he shouted as loudly as he could. He was angry at himself, and with himself. But what happened?

The old man leapt up a second time, weeping even more loudly. He was almost hysterical.

"Don't! Please don't shout at me! I'll go. I will, I promise. But don't shout at me. I've been shouted at often enough in my long life. I will go. I promise. I always go whenever anyone shouts at me ..."

"I'll go, I promise I will ..." he whispered, crying, as he walked away.

Our hero was livid. Absolutely furious. It was all his own fault. He pulled his hair. He leapt about, doing judo kicks to the right and left. He beat his breast, his knees, his head.

Still he was not satisfied. There had to be another way to punish himself. There had to. He picked up a large rock ...

"Don't do it!" the old man suddenly shouted, much to our

hero's surprise.

"Don't do what?"

"Don't do it! Don't do it!"

"By all the gods, don't do what, sir?"

The old man continued sobbing.

"Don't do it ... please don't do it ..."

Our hero was sorry. He threw the rock away. Of course the old man was stopping him from bashing his own head in. Actually the "Don't do it" was part of the old man's lament "Don't do it! Please don't shout at me ...". Consequently a large rock had been forbidden to play its role in a confused attempt at suicide, in a confused, weary, dark corner of the earth ...

"How difficult it is for two human beings to communicate with each other," thought our hero.

"Sir! Please, sir!"

The cry was like a knife. It tore through the darkness and silence of the night. Its pathos tore through the old man's heart. It was like the final cry of a person about to be taken by a wave or lost in a fire.

The old man was startled by its pain and agony. He turned around in the dark.

He was surprised. Very surprised. He could hear a young man crying. Howling.

"Oh!" he thought. "I'd better not stop him. Let him finish first. If you stop someone crying, all sorts of unexpected complications can happen. Some sorts of crying can be soothed with soft words. But that's dangerous with other types. If I tried coaxing him, it would be like pouring petrol on a fire. He would be worse. Something terrible might follow. He might try to harm me. Or he might run amok and try to hurt himself. People have been known to try to kill their comforters with the first thing they can lay their hands on. Even smash their heads against brick walls ..."

Soon our hero's weeping lessened.

"Sir!"

"Yes, what is it?"

Silence. Our hero was embarrassed. "He knows I've been crying," he thought.

"Can we talk about something else, my son? I find our conversation very wearing. In all my years, I don't think I have ever taken part in such mind-destroying talk. I'm too old to do so now."

Our hero was amazed.

"But, sir! You started it!"

"Yes. But you ought also to remind yourself that it was your answer that confirmed its serious nature."

Our hero laughed. And when he heard the laugh, humanity being what it is, the old man had to join in.

Our hero guffawed. The old man giggled.

The explosive laughter of two men smashed the darkness and silence of night into a thousand shattered pieces. Two men, caught helplessly in a very small part of a very large drought, with its harsh suffering and emptiness ...

They wanted to talk like normal human beings. What do normal human beings talk about? What do they say? How is it different from abnormal human conversation?

They were silent. Their tongues were like mud. They could not seem to talk at all ...

"How difficult it is to communicate," they thought. "To do ordinary things. To talk normally ..."

Should they try not to talk at all? Then what about human communication? What would happen to man if ...

Our hero decided to leave. Walk on.

The old man decided to leave. Walk on.

Our hero walked quickly away. The old man walked slowly and awkwardly away.

Soon the area was deserted. It was again simply the middle of a road. A slice of road to: onwards.

Tomorrow, or perhaps the day after, one man might meet another man there, they might talk seriously, they might not. We seldom remember the precise place where we met a particular person, did a certain thing, yet that person, that thing, can never fully be erased from our lives.

Usually we think of a road as a means of connecting one place with another, and not as a collection of various sections, each possessed of its own universe.

Roads have to do with traffic. Economics. Demography. Urbanisation and rural development. Political leadership and the modern state. Fools have tried to analyse highway psychology. Some have even tried to find poetry there; these are no ordinary people. They are a-social, eccentric, and take little interest in normal human intercourse ...

The first rays of dawn shone like ash-white lines. It was again possible to distinguish between the edge of the road and the bald hills in the distance.

But still he had seen nothing like a town. Or a village. Or a house. Or even a hut. Or anything else.

He had not even heard the crow of a rooster!

He wondered where the subdistrict capital was. Its name had been clearly displayed on the notice-board and he had read it, yesterday — or the day before — or some time. To hell with when exactly, but he had read it.

How many kilometers had he walked? He wagered he had been walking for at least twenty hours. At an average five kilometers an hour. So at least a hundred kilometers. And still he had not come to the town, not even a ghost town.

Towns do not usually display their names a hundred kilometers away. Except at airports. He had seen signboards showing towns thousands, even tens of thousands, of miles away. Airlines used that sort of thing in their advertising too. The passengers liked it.

Placing the signboard to a small town — let alone to a subdistrict capital — hundreds of kilometers away is a joke in very bad taste indeed. It is not in the least funny.

Scratching his head, our hero kept on walking. To be honest, he was beginning to feel tired. Everything felt heavy. His eyes. His feet. He needed to sleep.

"No!" he snapped. "I have many needs. If I give in to one of them, I will probably want to give in to them all. I can't take the risk. They would all come flocking, pushing each other along. The need for food and drink, to live an ordinary life, have a calling-card, a house, a house number, a telephone, a telephone number, money, a bank account, a codename for cables and telex, a large iron fence around my house, with a metal plate that says 'Beware of the dog!', a wife and children, an album for photographs of the family, tax and insurance, a family doctor and a regular newspaper, favourite film and radio stars, certain political and social allegiances, to certain political and social groups, my own blood-group, my own corner of the house and garden, and so on and so on.

To hell with that!"

He walked.

Walked.

Walked. Without stopping.

In the empty world of the early morning.

Completely empty.

Empty. Endlessly.

At midday he arrived at a hamlet. Old, tall houses on pillars, with shingle and corrugated iron roofs. The yards were bare. As bare and as dry as the surrounding district.

"What a strange village!" thought our hero.

Several thin, low-bellied dogs wandered underneath the houses. Dogs. Nothing else.

There were no people. None.

Our hero coughed. Loudly. Several times.

Nobody put his head out to see who was coughing. Even the dogs ignored him. They continued roaming, aimlessly. They were not even interested in barking at him.

Our hero walked between the houses. Strange! All the doors and windows were wide open. Gaping at the world. There was nobody inside.

Recklessly he climbed the ladder to one house. It was empty. He entered other houses. They were all still-life paintings of ordinary village houses with ordinary village furniture.

Suddenly he smelt food. He had not eaten since leaving the hospital.

Quickly he ran to where the smell was coming from. It was true. There was something more or less like a cupboard and it contained rice, vegetables and several pieces of fried salted-fish. The food was still luke-warm. Which meant it had recently been cooked. That was true too. The firewood was still smoking in the kitchen.

Then someone must live in the house. Perhaps he or she had

stepped out for a moment. Somewhere. Certainly not far. He or she — or they — would soon be back. For the food.

"I'd better wait," thought our hero. He fought off his hunger. Licking his dry lips, he climbed down the ladder once more.

He was stunned. There was a man with a large bushy beard standing at the bottom of the steps. He screamed.

The man with the beard screamed too. Our hero's scream surprised him.

"He'll kill me!" thought our hero. "He's as big as an ox. I'm as thin as a stick. I'll be black and blue — one blow and I'll collapse. Still, I'll fight as hard as I can! I'm no dead fish, yet."

"Come on!" thought our hero. "If he wants to start something, let him!" He closed his eyes and took up a defensive stance ...

The Beard led him up the ladder and into the house.

"Welcome," he said. He sat our hero down on a mat. Then he offered him food.

"Eat up!"

Our hero was staggered.

"What about you? Are you going to eat too?"

"You first. I'm not sure whether there's enough for myself or not. If there isn't, I'll cook something later. You start, please."

Our hero was dazed. "Am I really about to eat? To eat real food? Not just food in a dream — a dream that is as old as the drought?"

"Hell!" the Beard suddenly exploded. "Stop pretending. You're not in town now. Do you want to eat, or don't you? Even the dogs can see how hungry you are. You're thinner than them. Eat up! If you don't, I will!"

His dizziness and reluctance vanished with the first mouthfull. So did his hesitation. Slowly but surely he gorged himself.

As he did so, the Beard cooked.

"There's more here, if you haven't got enough."

"No thank you. There's plenty here."

The Beard looked at him in disbelief.

"All you city folk are the same! Polite to the end, despite the fact you're dying."

He laughed loudly. A huge, deep, bass laugh.

"Honestly you know, I like it when people are polite. Civilised." He laughed again.

"The swine!" cursed our hero to himself. "He's so crude. He not only looks prehistoric, he behaves like it as well. But ... you know, I like it when people are barbaric."

After he had finished eating, the Beard said: "I don't care who you are, where you come from, or where you are going. You could be on the run from the police. Or a political refugee. A tramp or a member of a spiritual order. An uncreative, bored writer. Not that I can see much difference between any of them. What you are is entirely your own business. There's only one thing I want to say: 'If you want to go, now that you've eaten, you're quite welcome to do so. On the other hand, if you want to stay a while, or longer, or forever, you're welcome to do that too. It's up to you.' "

"How strange," thought our hero. "Another strange man. The drought seems to breed them."

"I think I'll stay. For a while anyway. Then I'll see what I want to do after that."

"It's entirely up to you, I told you."

"Who is he?" wondered our hero. "His manner is so blunt. But he doesn't offend me in the least."

"There is one thing. I know it's up to me. But I must know what you think too."

"Tell me," replied the Beard, calmly. He began to eat the food he had cooked.

"What will I eat, if I stay? I haven't brought anything."

The Beard laughed. Several grains of rice leapt from his mouth.

"I think I'm going to like you. You're so honest."

After the next mouthful, he drank. Then he finished eating.

"Up to a few months ago I was leader of a troop of bandits. I formed the band several years back, using various political slogans I picked up here and there. Not that I believed them all, of course. But I felt that the upper classes had betrayed the armed revolution by ending it too quickly, and I wanted an outlet for my frustration. I wasn't used to peace and quiet. I had given everything to the Revolution. A deliberate gamble. I even gave up my ability to adjust to difficult situations. It wasn't hard to find experienced, like-minded friends. They were a lethal lot — strong adult males, sharing the same frustrations, the same anxieties and the same loneliness. None of them believed in the political basis of our struggle either. We soon moved on to the sort of deed the law considers evil. It wasn't much of a step. Theft, robbery, arson, murder, rape. These became our principles. We worked at them day after day, month after month, year after year. Work was an escape from loneliness and anxiety. We were happy! You could tell that by the way the government had to keep finding new terms to describe us: vicious, savage, inhuman, God only knew what else. But there was one thing we hadn't reckoned on. Even the fiercest, cruelest bunch of thugs eventually gets bored. Army troops get bored with war, tired of killing, we got tired too. Robbery, murder, rape and arson became boring. The men's morale declined, one by one. They became too lazy to run away and died one by one. They deliberately let the government troops catch them, one by one. Some even ran and surrendered, begging to be pardoned. One day only the core of the band was left. The best of the bunch. They came to me and asked me:

'What do we do next?'

I told them:

'It's up to you. Anyone who wants to go, can go. I won't stop him.'

'We're thinking of surrendering. Will you join us?'

'I certainly will not. What I do from now on is entirely my own business. I won't let anyone else interfere.'

'How about swearing an oath? Together we live and die?'

'We did that when we started. Do you want to use the oath of unity to disband?'

'So you won't join us?'

'You won't join me, you mean.'

The discussion concluded with a short, sharp exchange of shots. I was amazed. I had killed them all. I couldn't believe it. I looked at their bodies, one by one, and their weapons; none of them had tried to hit me. The first shot was just to provoke me. To make me shoot them. They had worked it out very shrewdly. On the one hand they didn't want to surrender to the army, on the other hand they were getting more and more bored. That was one set of problems. There was another one, which was harder still. They didn't want to commit suicide. As it turned out, they didn't kill themselves, officially anyway. They were killed. By me. I found a letter in one of their pockets, explaining the whole thing. It was a farewell letter ..."

The Beard's voice cracked. There were tears in the corners of his eyes. He gulped a beaker of water down. Then coughed. Loudly. Several times.

"My nose is running. I think I'm getting the flu."

He wiped his eyes and blew his nose several times unnecessarily.

Once his "influenza" had diminished, he continued:

"I buried them under these houses."

"Here?" screamed our hero.

"Yes, here. They used to live here."

"So I'm in ..."

"... a bandit hide-out."

"A bandit hide-out!"

"To be precise: a former bandit hide-out. One man can't be a bandit on his own. Listen to it: band-it. With the best will in the world, he can't be a bandit without there being others too. And to answer your other question: Don't worry about food. The houses are full of food. There was enough food for the whole band for at least two months. I don't think I need explain where it came from."

Our hero nodded. He could guess.

"What about water?"

"That's a bit more difficult, I agree."

"How do you mean?"

"The drought. All the wells have dried up."

"All of them?"

"No, fortunately not all. Two still give water. Every day I go and look at them. See those pitchers in the yard? I get them filled daily."

"Who fills them?"

"The dogs do. They used to be hunting dogs. I trained them to do this. They also help me in other ways as well."

"Who made the pitchers?"

"I did. With local clay. It's one of the things I do each day."

The Beard look mischievously at our hero for a while. Then he said:

"Don't worry. There's enough food and drink for both of us for a while. And I don't intend asking you to help me form a new band. Even if you wanted to, two people don't make a band either."

He laughed.

Our hero did not.

"I used to be a bandit."

"What?"

His face changed, as though he had suddenly seen a ghost in broad daylight. He stared at our hero.

"Whether you believe me or not is your business. The fact is: I used to be a bandit."

He told his story. About his part in the Revolution. The end of the armed struggle. The return to normality. Peace. His inability to readjust to peace and normality. How he had met other friends who also felt restless and isolated. How they became a terrorist band. How he was caught during a fight. And condemned to death. About his former subordinates, now judge and prosecutor. The light sentence he had received. His pardon. About the lectures he had followed in philosophy and history. How bored he was. His leaving the university. Transmigrating. The destruction of the transmigrant settlement by the drought. His struggle against the drought and the open conflict between them. His temporary defeat. How he burnt the settlement down. His collapse and transfer to a psychiatric ward. How he left the hospital. His meeting his friend, now no longer a transmigrant but the leader of a counterfeiting and smuggling ring. His refusal to join and become second-in-command to Al Capone. About the unpaved road he had followed. His strange meeting and conversation with an old man whom he could not see and did not know. And very last of all: how he had met a man with a big beard, who was stranger than anyone else he had ever met in his whole life. And absolutely last of all: the discovery that he was in a bandit hide-out, and that the man with a beard and the build of Adam in paradise had also led a gang of bandits, and was no different from himself ...

As he listened, the Beard could not stop laughing. His laughter stabbed through the secret quiet around them, like lightning through a drought sky. The dogs stiffened and paused as they wandered around the yard. Then they took to their heels and ran, without making a sound.

The old unpainted house seemed to shake as well.

Once his laughter had diminished, he patted our hero on the shoulder.

"I thought I was going to like you. I do like you."

Our hero shuddered. What did he mean? 'Like?' He hoped that the Beard wasn't a homosexual ...

"My friend, I salute you. Take the hand of a colleague. The hand of one outlaw freely offered to another. I take it I won't upset you if I shout: 'Long live all former bandits!' And 'Bandits of the world unite — no matter what you are or what you believe!' "

"You aren't really a former bandit."

"Why not?"

"You've never surrendered to the authorities. You've never been captured, never even been beaten. So you're still on duty. Still an enlisted bandit, so to speak."

"Oh to hell with your bureaucratic ways. Look at it this way: one man on his own can't be a bandit. And even if he could, if he doesn't want to be called a bandit, he isn't a bandit. Compare the situation to that of a terrorist: how can anyone be a terrorist if he doesn't terrorise anyone? Impossible! A bandit isn't like a university graduate, with B.Eng., M.Ec., LL.B., D.V.Sc., D.D.S., B.A., M.A., etc, after his name for the rest of his life. Longer, in fact — 'Here lies Professor Dr. So-and-so M.A.' ... He's more like a book-keeper. When a book-keeper stops keeping books, he stops being a book-keeper. Or, when a motor-mechanic stops fixing cars, he isn't a motor mechanic anymore. At best, he's a superannuated motor mechanic. Assuming he receives superannuation. Or an ex-motor mechanic. In that sense, I am an ex-bandit. So are you. Our friends who have, or will have, surrendered to the government, are ex-bandits as well."

Our hero was impressed by this admirable exposition. "What an unusual ex-bandit," he thought. "The sort of strangeness I like. Good. I think we're going to be good friends.''

He took the Beard's hand.

''Friend, I salute you. Long live all ex-bandits! Bandits of the world unite!''

The Beard was startled. But he quickly joined in with a thunderous cheer:

''Hip! Hip! hurr-ay! Long live all ex-bandits!''

The cheers stabbed through the afternoon sky and echoed on the bald hills in the distance.

Twilight came in transparent orange slices. Orange like afternoon drought. The endless drought.

SIX

One day the second last well ran dry. The dogs, who had come for water, barked at the dry hole. Then they barked at the crisp sky. Then they ran yelping to announce the catastrophe to our two heroes.

The Beard and our hero came running, as fast as deer. They looked at each other in silence. And went to the last spring.

"Things will be even more serious when the last well dries up!" announced the Beard, like a god in some Greek tragedy proclaiming the consequences of a natural disaster. "But we've stored a lot of water already, haven't we? So why should we worry?"

They climbed up the bank and back to the village.

"The real problem isn't whether we've stored enough water or not. It's the tension and the sense of walking the edge of a deep ravine that we get from the drought. The next stage will be far more serious: the worry of whether we can physically and mentally survive the next stages. The next stages will be even more tense and serious. The tension won't come from water and the drought, but from life itself, and from the ultimate limits of our endurance. Can we live despite the uncertainty of life? Despite death? When the drought ends, the well won't matter. It will be just another well and of no great dramatic significance. But because God has chosen to play with the weather, and doesn't care about us, then the well is something of immense existential concern. It is no longer a well but: Our future! Without it we have no future, despite all our jars ..."

The community carried on its daily life. There were seven citizens: two people and five dogs. Each one did the work he had agreed to do.

They took it in turns to cook. There was less need to make pots, now that there was only one well. The dogs — consequently — had more time to sleep under the houses.

"I've never seen dogs bored before," said our hero after spending the whole day watching them.

The Beard laughed.

"They're no different from humans. When they're bored, they sleep. Then they get bored with that and start fighting. Eventually that gets boring too. They eat, until they are no longer interested in eating. Then they sleep again, until they lose interest in that too."

"You mean they're too bored to live?"

"I think so. Except that their civilisation hasn't yet reached the level where they can debate suicide as an escape from boredom."

"You said that you thought they would fight until they're too bored to fight. Do you think we'll do that?"

"Fight, you mean?"

"Yes."

"It's quite possible."

The Beard laughed.

"But we've got something the dogs haven't. We can talk about the problem before it happens. Which makes it less likely to happen. The full structure of our awareness is based on the following premises: (1) human beings know when they are bored, (2) they know they can fight, (3) they know they shouldn't fight. That is human civilisation, in sum."

"What if we do fight ...?"

"That will make things difficult. We might fight because we know we can fight ..."

They laughed.

"The dogs have been fighting a lot more these last few days. Haven't you noticed?"

"I have. It's probably because the last bitch died two weeks ago. They need another one."

"Why did she die?"

"She wasn't strong enough to please them all. Boredom can turn into lust too. I don't think she thought much about love. She had to share herself with four brutes, none of whom she cared for. Her Romeo was too weak to face four rivals endowed by fate with far stronger muscles and sharper teeth."

Our hero listened to the Beard's words as if in a dream.

"Sex is the most serious problem any guerrilla or outlaw group has to face. While I was a leader I made it a firm policy that there should never be any women around. A woman's presence is the seed of destruction.''

''How did you handle your own sexual needs?''

''I had the same needs as any other man. To be honest: Many of our operations were sexually motivated. We wanted to find women. You can imagine how ferocious we were when we didn't find any in a village. We burnt down innocent people's houses, mosques, and grain stores. We gave ourselves to the devil to satisfy our needs. The burning houses, piles of corpses and rivers of blood were simply substitutes. It was a vicious cycle. We never found any women. So we turned to other means of selfgratification. Which meant that we were even less satisfied. The more dissatisfied we felt, the greater the need for substitute gratification. We burnt more houses. Killed more people. Shed more blood. Sex lies at the basis of every bandit activity. Every bandit veniality. The problem is universal. It is part of every war and revolution. Except that the victors are not called bandits. Historians call them noble heroes. Nationalism recognises no heights greater than patriotism and courage.''

''I'm shocked at your cynicism! Your very words and sentences are boobytrapped. But you can't out-manoeuvre me like that. You still haven't answered my question. How did you handle your sexual needs when you were a bandit?''

The Beard laughed.

''I can see you're not an easy man to fool. All right, I'll tell you. I said before that I didn't know whether I could control my desire or not. What would any normal man do under the same circumstances? Without a woman? If I wanted to find one, I would have to leave. If I left (a) I would leave for the old reason, robbery, or (b) there would be another reason — in terms of the alternatives open to me — which was, to allow the army to capture me. In other words, I would be surrendering. Under these terms, I finally decided there were only two choices: sexual satisfaction or being taken alive by the army. You may not believe this, you may even think it fantastic, but: I wasn't ready to be taken alive. I liked things the way they were. The situation was obscure, perhaps even metaphysical ... but in either of these latter cases, I would have non-activated my outlaw status. There I was, a former bandit, with no clear concept of what I should be."

"Nonsense! An ex-bandit is still human. And an ex-outlaw of your standing would certainly have sexual needs."

"Nobody ever said that I didn't."

"So you admit it?"

"Of course I do."

"At last. Now stop trying to avoid the question. What did you do about them?"

"What does a hungry man do if he doesn't have any food?"

"Don't tell me you fasted, I won't believe that."

"What do you want me to say? Manual adultery — masturbation?"

Our hero was silent. He was embarrassed at having been caught thinking dirty thoughts.

The Beard laughed.

"You used to be a bandit, so you should know how prevalent manual adultery and homosexuality is among bands. Every bandit is, by definition, a masturbator, and both an active and passive homosexual. Although I wouldn't say that everyone actually practised such things."

"It's the exception that proves the rule!"

"True! But don't forget the nuances contained in that statement. The exception, the special case, shouldn't be sacrified for the sake of the masses."

"What do you mean?"

"The exception exists. It should not be ignored, neither should it be obliterated."

"Do you think your sexual needs make you a special case?"

"Yes. In as far as my abilities are no greater than anyone else's."

"Do you mean you're impotent?"

"My god! What is this? An inquisition?"

"Are you impotent?"

"Probably."

"How can you tell?"

"I don't have any definite evidence. To really tell, I'd have to find a woman ..."

"So you don't really know?"

"Can you bring me a woman so that I can find out?"

"How did you decide you're impotent?"

"I have no sexual drive."

"Of course not. There aren't any women here."

"I don't even have fantasies about beautiful naked women. If I did, I might feel stimulated. I might ..."

"... commit manual adultery!"

"Yes."

"But there are other, more sublime, forms of masturbation."

"I know what you mean. I can't."

"I beg your pardon?"

"I'm not a creative artist, a poet."

"Have you tried?"

"Either one is a poet or one isn't. You can't become a poet. That's stupid. There's only one thing more stupid, and that's trying to become a poet."

"Many poets have become poets because they wanted to."

"I know that."

"Their poems are admired. Even by people who are born poets.

"I know that."

"Don't you think this is the ideal setting and time to test whether you have talent or not?"

"What do you mean 'ideal'?"

"The best poetry is written after long periods of intense self-conflict. And of course there is another, very important factor: you're a failure."

The Beard was silent. His anger mounted. He wanted to hit our hero in the face. But he quickly controlled himself. A forced smile hovered on his lips.

"Hey! It's my turn to cook, isn't it. We've been so busy talking we've forgotten how hungry we are. Ha! Ha! ha!"

He leapt down the ladder and ran to the kitchen.

Our hero was bitterly sorry. So he had finally said it. 'A failure'. It was like ripping a sword out of a sheath. The sword had two edges. One faced the Beard, the other ... himself.

Few people had fought the term as determinedly or as vocally as he had. Every stage of his life was marked with a large unpainted board bearing the letters painted in tar: F-A-I-L-U-R-E.

Failure had reigned over him from the time he was in the womb. Or in his father's sperm. From the earliest period in his childhood he could remember. He had never been able to mix with children of his own age. He had never even felt close to his toys. He couldn't bear to look at himself in the mirror. He couldn't share other people's joys and grief. No one ever cared how he felt. He didn't know how to talk to girls, to get a girlfriend, or to propose. Women never responded to him, loved him, wanted to sleep with him, or to accept his seed and allow it grow into an outward manifestation of desire.

In short, he had every qualification, skill and talent necessary to be a failure. But everyone thought he was ideal. He was handsome. He was sociable. Everyone said he was helpful, friendly and a good conversationalist. He was highly intelligent. His friends and teachers all admired him.

But so far his abundant skill and talents had made him no more than almost a success. And because near success is, basically, no success at all, everything he did was unsuccessful, alias a failure.

The war had broken out just before he completed his studies in history and philosophy. Just as he had almost made a fortune as a blackmarketeer and a forger of counterfeit money, thanks to his connections with the Japanese troops, the war ended and the Revolution began. Just as he was about to reclaim a town from the enemy and thus completely reconquer the whole sector under his command, the armed struggle ended. Just as he was about to be appointed regimental commander, he decided to go to the hills and form his own band of terrorists. Just when he had almost succeeded in attacking and occupying a town held by the government, he had been shot, wounded, and captured. Just as he was about to be sentenced to death, he was pardoned. Just as he was about to graduate at last, he became a nuisance, led a minor campus revolt, and then left the university forever. Just as he had almost succeeded in becoming a transmigrant farmer, the dry season turned into prolonged outrageous drought.

This was his story. One failure after another. Failure was the fundamental essence of his whole existence.

But he never dared say the word. For years it had terrorised his every utterance. It lay in wait behind his every word and sentence, ready to leap out and shout at him. He was frightened to talk.

He was like Prometheus carrying an enormous rock of failure. Each action was a reaction to the word. He was obsessed with its possible presence at any moment in time ...

But, as always happens, the word was a boomerang. It frightened him and he tried hard to avoid it, but he saw it in every atom of air he breathed.

And now it had pierced the very axis of his being.

He was a failure ...

There was only one well. They didn't need many pots. What else was there to do?

The dogs fought constantly. The noise forced him to a quick decision.

He found the Beard damping down the fire.

"I'm going."

The Beard was stunned.

"Where?"

"I don't know."

"Why?"

"I don't want to be like the dogs."

The Beard nodded.

"A woman?"

Our hero nodded.

"I understand."

After a moment's silence he added:

"I'm coming too."

"Really?"

"Sure. You're my friend. I don't want to lose you."

"Stop fooling about."

"No, things have been different while you've been here. I couldn't stand the silence again."

"What are you going to do?"

"Help you find a woman."

"And then what?"

"We'll bring her back."

"You mean steal a woman?"

"Kidnap her, to be precise."

"But we're not bandits any more."

"If I have to be to make you stay, I'll try. One last time, I hope. I'll even go on my own, if necessary."

"We can both go. But ..."

"But what?"

"What if the army catches you?"

"I'll shave my beard off. If I am recognised and taken prisoner ..." He shrugged. "That's a risk I'll have to take. There's only one other alternative, letting you go, and I don't want to do that."

"So you've changed your position?"

"There's a limit to the silence and loneliness any man can suffer ..."

Once they had shaved and changed their clothes, they left. They provided three days food for the dogs in nine tins. It was enough for nine meals. The dogs ate three times a day. During their absence the dogs would still have to work filling the jars with water from the one well.

They were not scavenger dogs for nothing. They were as shrewdly calculating as any partisan.

What if the Beard and his friend didn't return in three days? They weren't worried. They knew the risks partisans took. Hunger or death — starvation, or a bullet from an army patrol.

What if the well dried up? They weren't worried. They would survive, they knew the rules. No water to carry and store? Then no need to carry water. No food to eat? Then no need to eat. Loss of life? No need to worry. They would die. Survival, neither dead nor alive? No need to worry. They wouldn't die, neither would they live. What does one call this state of being neither alive nor dead? God knows. What's in a name? Basically they would live as long as they could, to the last moment of life — death — appointed them.

"Why did you bring your pistol?" asked our hero, when the village was far behind them.

"Oh, habit. You can never tell when you might need it."

"But our mission is to find a woman. Not to shoot one."

"What if we're forced to shoot?"

"How, for example?"

"In self-defence."

"People who are quick on the draw always plead self-defence."

"Shall I throw it away?"

Our hero was startled.

"No! Are you mad?"

"Well, what do you want me to do?"

Our hero snatched the gun and caressed its cold black steel. His eyes shone with snatches of an old tale. He did not say what it was.

"You look after it," said the Beard, once he had recognized the gleam in our hero's eyes.

They walked. Two strong men walking, walking, walking, the way that men who knew nothing else walked. Men who ate, pissed, slept, walking. They had to walk, walk, walk, whether they wanted to or not. If they didn't want to, the army would kill them. For the army was also comprised of men whose job it was, day after day, to walk, walk, walk. Walking men, pursued by walking men ...

They reached town the next morning. The same town our hero had started from. The same town he had been hospitalised in. The same town that his friend lived in, the little fat man, leader of an international smuggling and counterfeiting organisation.

"Where are we going?" asked the Beard.

Our hero shook his head.

"You must know!"

"Towns always confuse me. I never know where I want to go. There are always too many roads, too many directions to follow."

"What should we do next?"

"I don't know. The only thing is that we came ..."

"... to get a woman. Perhaps some coffee-stall owner in the mountains who has come to town for coffee, sugar, tobacco and salted fish."

"I never know how to do anything. I just know that I have to do it."

"The method is the same, whether you have to or not."

"I usually let things work themselves out."

"Like a bull in a china shop?"

"Not at all! There's always a plan. But you have to wait for it to come. It'll come when you need it."

"This time there are two of us. Me and you. Or, you and me. We should work things out properly if we're going to succeed. We ought to think about things."

Our hero laughed.

"Work out our strategy. Is that what you mean?"

They laughed.

"And what comes before strategy?"

"Logistics, if I'm not mistaken."

"Right!" shouted the Beard. "Including the problem of accomodation."

"We can stay where all travellers stay: in a hotel."

"You need identification to stay in a hotel."

"Haven't you got any?"

"If you mean forged papers, of course I've got some."

They laughed.

"That's just the problem."

"What do you mean?"

"They're too good. Its always the same: the better the forgery — in other words, the less it looks like a forgery — the more I worry."

"We won't go to a hotel then. Do you have any other suggestions?"

"No."

They laughed.

"Did I ever tell you about my friend the smuggler? What about staying with him?"

The Beard agreed. They went there.

The VIP girl — the little fat man's mistress — greeted them warmly.

"You devil!" whispered the Beard, nudging our hero.

The little fat man was not at home. He was away. On official business. But he had given the VIP explicit instructions to prepare for our hero while he was away.

"For me?"

"Yes. He was sure you'd be back."

Our hero was furious. How dare the little fat man assume that he would come back, especially as he had. And the woman said it so calmly.

His anger did not last long. The two men watched her as she led them into the house.

"We can share a room," insisted our hero when the VIP showed them to separate rooms.

"Certainly not!" she insisted. "As I am the lady of the house, I shall decide who stays where. You wouldn't want to argue with your hostess, would you?"

She pinched his cheek mischievously.

"On my god!" whispered the Beard, nudging our hero.

"You'll understand why you have separate rooms later on ..." she giggled.

Then she showed them the bathrooms, the toilets, cupboards full of clothing, which bell to push if they needed absolutely anything at all, the telephones, the library, and the armoury.

"Tremendous!" whispered the Beard, nudging our hero.

After they had washed and changed their clothes — choosing what they wanted from the extensive range provided — they ate. The Beard whispered:

"I don't think this is going to take long."

Our hero was shocked.

"Do you mean our hostess?"

The Beard nodded firmly.

"Impossible. She belongs to my friend."

"Women are all the same. They belong to everyone, or they belong to no one."

Our hero was temporarily silent.

"We need more than one woman anyway."

"We?"

"Well, we didn't come just for my sake."

"A woman is of no use to me."

"That remains to be seen."

"I'm too scared to find out."
"One isn't enough."
"It's not too many, not too few. I don't need anyone."
"You're not writing a novel about a three-sided love affair, are you?"
"I've already told you I'm not a creative writer."
"I refuse!"
"Why?"
"It's not natural. Two men and only one woman..."
"You mean one normal man and one other ..."
"Until the reverse is proven, I consider you as healthy as any other Casanova. I know what you're like. I've got an idea: I think I'll put you to the test ..."
The Beard chuckled.
"Don't waste your time!"
"Would you mind?"
"Be my guest."
Our hero looked at the Beard for a long time.
"Shall we start with our hostess?" our hero asked.
"Our hostess? Don't be depraved. Anyway, she belongs to your friend."
"He's my friend, not yours."
"Any friend of yours is a friend of mine."
"She's a woman. And by the look of her ... wow! fantastic in bed!"
They chuckled.
"I could do it with her! Hell, I could do it with anyone! I'm ready, put me to the test!"
They laughed.

They spent the afternoon walking around the town. The Beard had to struggle to control the overwhelming rush of his own sensations. It had been a long time since he was last in a town and he seemed to be waking slowly from a very long, hideous nightmare. Everything he saw seemed wrapped in impenetrable mystery. He felt as though he had just landed on another planet, after a long journey through outer space.

Our hero was aware of his friend's feelings. He left him alone as far as possible. The same experience had once been his.

He wondered whether a man like the Beard could ever re-adjust to the city. A city is not like the mountains. Especially as bandits know the mountains. Cold, the mist full of suspicion and treachery, fear, hunger and the final reaches of man's ability to suffer. There is no rustle of voices. Except the very occasional sound of an exchange of shots and the cry of the dead before they breathe their last. Compared to battle in other places, mountain fighting sounds very tired and sad. Miserable. The men fall like dumb throttled animals. They have learnt to suffer and die in silence. They die in silence and are buried — if they are buried — without comment.

Even gibbons have to accept the stifling silence. Those that hoot a lot at sunset are driven out by their companions — or leave of their own accord — and move to another forest, where there are no bandits. The revolutionary movement is spreading throughout the world, most forests seem to support a revolutionary band. The monkeys that can't find satisfactory shelter will eventually die. Of exhaustion. Wandering from one terrorist sector to another.

Of all the things in town, the Beard was undoubtedly most upset by women. There are few women in the mountains. Those there are, are not like those found in the city. Most mountain women do not have red lips, full breasts and long curly hair. Nor do they give off perfume from their casually passing bodies. That was the most intense of all sensations and it made the Beard reel.

"Let's sit down for a while."

Our hero led the Beard to the nearest coffee stall.

"I suggest we complete our mission as quickly as possible."

"What's wrong?"

"I can't take much more."

"All right. But this walking is part of our mission as well."

"Then hurry up and make your choice."

"Choice?"

"Choose your victim."

"So far we've only talked about women in the abstract, haven't we?"

'As long as it's a woman, who cares?"

"You're right."

"Good. We're leaving tomorrow."

"That's too quick."

"Is there anything else we should do?"

"No."

"Tomorrow at the latest. We could go tonight, if you'd let me fix things up the way I wanted."

Our hero said nothing. He paid for the drinks. They left.

"We could even go before night-time."

"You agreed to my suggestion."

"Which suggestion?"

"That I put you to the test. I regard this as a matter of great principle. If you win, we only need one woman. If you're wrong, then the object of our mission becomes: two women."

"I'll second that!" shouted the Beard.

There was another woman there when they arrived back at the house.

Young, beautiful, well-built.

"You devil!" whispered the Beard, nudging our hero.

They smiled and their hostess made the introductions.

"What's she doing here?" our hero asked impatiently.

The hostess mischievously pinched his cheek.

"I've given you separate rooms. I think it's sufficiently obvious why she is here."

Our hero shivered.

"Oh! Is that why?"

"Two for two should be enough. Or would you like four?" She giggled.

"That makes things hard," thought our hero. "So it's one against one tonight. The problem is who gets who?" He was not a hard man to please but, to be honest, he hoped he didn't have to make love to his hostess. He couldn't. He knew his etiquette. Both in the East and the West, one's duty was to respect one's hostess.

It was an old problem. No matter how much he loved or desired a woman, his passion vanished as soon as he learnt she was related to one of his friends, or an acquaintance of an acquaintance. The class of forbidden women included: landladies' daughters, nurses who cared for him while he was in hospital, class-mates, women employed as typists in the university administration, women at the post office where he went to cash the postal note his parents sent him every two months to pay for his board, all the girls who lived in the same lane or street as himself.

Any such tie completely put the brakes on his desire. In fact it even created a sort of Oedipus complex as far as he was concerned.

If they had to face the two women that night, one against one, he hoped from the very bottom of his heart that he wouldn't get the gracious lady of the house ...

"That would be like having intercourse with one's sister!" he snapped at himself.

After the usual subsequent trifles, they discussed the evening's program: bed. The VIP briefly reminded them of their absent host's instructions that our hero must be satisfied in every respect. He must lack nothing. She wanted to make sure that that was the case, and hoped that he would enjoy all that was offered to him.

The brief introduction over, the hostess announced the pairings: the Beard with the newcomer, and ... the rest was obvious.

Our hero felt his knees collapse under him.

"Would you like to change with me?" whispered the Beard, when he saw how pale our hero was.

"I really would. But it wouldn't be polite."

"To hell with etiquette! To hell with culture! Women are all the same. Treat her the way you'd treat any other woman. Don't waste your opportunity. Goodnight."

The newcomer, already dressed in a transparent night gown, was waiting for him at the door of the bedroom. She promptly swept him into her arms, and — like a giant octopus — dragged him in, kicking the door shut with her foot.

Later that night, two doors opened simultaneously. The two women ran out. Their clothing was in complete disarray. They ran into the lounge, howling.

Soon two men appeared from the same two rooms. They seemed calm. Too calm. Noticing the two women in the lounge room, they went outside and sat on a bench.

Drought stars shone in the sky. Quietly. Very quietly.

The two men said nothing. The two women said nothing. They had stopped crying. They sat, as though in a state of shock.

The clock chimed four times. One woman began crying again. Sobbing loudly. At this, the other woman began sobbing too. Loudly.

One man stood up in the yard. He sighed. Then he began walking. Around the yard. At this, the other man stood. And sighed. As though trying to suck every star out of the sky. Then he too began walking, in the opposite direction to his friend.

A jet of white spray appeared in the sky. After a brief chat with the stars, it vanished.

Dawn had come.

The two women stopped crying. They sat silently in their chairs, stunned.

The two men sat down on the bench again. They looked at each other briefly. They sat. Silently. On the hard bench. Sternly.

The sky was preparing morning. In one large pot it boiled together the stars, the dew, sleep, dreams, hope, nostalgia, sleepless anxiety. The atmosphere changed. The temperature changed. The quality of the silence changed. The perfume in the air changed.

The post-dawn sky stank of man, and his fear.

The calm was shattered by a number of voices with no origin and no purpose. The sound of silence, now no longer tranquil ...

Finally the first golden rays perched in the eastern sky, enveloping everything briefly in gold. Then the gilding faded, and everything was the same as it had always been. The light steadily increased.

The sun was rising.

The first rays of sunlight perching on his nose woke the first man from his thoughts. He looked at the other man.

In silent accord they went back inside the house. They

washed. They dressed in the clothes they had arrived in. They ate the food the servant brought them. Then they looked at each other again.

In silent accord they went to the two women. The women were standing at the front door. They wanted to say goodbye to the two men.

The four people stood facing each other. No one spoke. They looked at each other. Deeply, lovingly.

Four smiles spread on four faces. Four hands held each other, tightly intimately.

The two men left. The two women escorted them to the gate.

They faced each other again. Still no one spoke. They looked at each other. Deeply, lovingly.

Four smiles spread on four morning faces. Four hands shook, holding each other tightly, intimately.

No one spoke.

Then the two men departed, forever. They took large, strong steps. Walking like men who knew nothing else in life but walking, walking, walking. They were humanity on the march.

When the two men were at last out of sight, one of the women began crying. At this, the other ditto.

Two women weeping, at the gate of morning.

They embraced each other, still weeping.

At last the stranglehold of silence was broken.

"The beast. I've never been so ashamed before in my whole life. No man has ever done what he did to me. Ugh! He didn't touch me. He just called me 'sister' and smiled. Nothing else."

The second woman was shaken by the depth of the first woman's grief. Her own pain forced her to confess.

"The same things happened to me too ..."

"But it's strange: he insulted me and I love him for it. I've never met anyone like him."

The second woman was dazed. She wiped her tears. Almost in a whisper she slowly admitted:

"The same thing happened to me. He's not like any other man I know. I think I've fallen in love with him. No matter how much he insulted me. I don't think I could ever love another man."

The first woman was stunned. She wiped her tears. She was very moved.

"I never thought," she whispered, "that I could fall in love. With any man. He told me about so many things: the dignity of womanhood, the place of woman in Eastern culture, etc. But he never touched me once."

The sun was planted high in the crystal-clear sky.

The morning freshness fell away, drop by drop, to be replaced by the oppressive heat. The drought.

Two tall men walking down a lonely unpaved road.

Neither of them said a word.

SEVEN

They arrived home to find that the day of judgement had preceded them:

(1) The last well was dry.

(2) The dogs were all dead. Their large gaping wounds suggested one final ferocious "all-in" fight.

(3) All the pots were broken, irrespective of whether they had held water or not. Presumably they were smashed during the fight.

(4) The houses were open — and absolutely bare.

"Now what do we do?" asked our hero.

They had buried the dogs and got rid of the broken potsherds.

"I don't know."

"There isn't anything we can do."

"True. Except live."

"Until we die of hunger and thirst."

"Don't be too sure. We might die some other way. Or even not die at all."

"Shall we pray?"

"Call it what you like. Praying. Or taking a chance, buying a ticket in a lottery."

"How much are the tickets?"

"You have to put in all the hope you have. For the drought to end."

"For the rain to fall!"

"The drought and rain are different. People don't suffer because of rain during the drought. All right. You've bought your ticket."

"What can we do until the prizes are drawn?"

"Live. That's work, isn't it?"

"The myth says that God kept working after Adam was created."

"That's not true. He worked for six days. Then he stopped. For a rest."

"What about us?"

"I suggest we start with the seventh day too."

"Rest?"

"Yes. The sixth day is over: We exist. Whether I like it or not, I exist. So let's start where God left off."

"In protest, you mean?"

"Call it what you like."

Our hero laughed.

"This conversation, intellectual as it is, doesn't help us understand the situation we find ourselves in."

"On the contrary. We wouldn't talk like this if we hadn't found ourselves in this situation."

"I've got an idea."

"What?"

"When we get really bored, let's try and find out who stole our food. Something worries me."

"What's that?"

"It happened while we weren't here."

"You're right."

They went and sat on the steps of one of the bare houses.

"Where do you want to start?" asked the Beard.

"We should try and work out who might have come."

"That's a hard question to answer."

"Why?"

"Anyone might have come."

"But you know the area better than anyone."

"That's what I mean."

"I beg your pardon?"

"A rebel doesn't 'know an area'. He fights an enemy. He knows the way the other side thinks. The way the army thinks. Logically. A bandit doesn't know his area, because he doesn't have an area. He can't unfold a map and say 'This is mine'. He never knows when the army has him in its sights."

Our hero was silent.

"Then we'd better stop. We'll never know."

"That's what I've been trying to tell you. In the mountains everything is possible. There are no guarantees. You live from one moment to the next. Live so that the next moment does actually come."

"To get back to the original question. The loss of our food can be explained in all sorts of ways. Someone robbed us. That's possible. The thief could have been anyone: a thief, a robber, or another group of terrorists, who may or may not share our ideology. Perhaps it was an army patrol. For them it would simply be a matter of strategy. An anti-guerrilla strike based on the premise that the most effective way of destroying enemy groups is to destroy their food and drink. But of course there are plenty of other possibilities as well."

"Such as?"

"The age of miracles has not yet finished."

"What do you mean by that?"

"The food may have vanished due to certain supernatural reasons beyond our comprehension."

"Poof — gone! Is that what you're saying?"

"Poof — gone!"

"Do you believe in that sort of thing?"

"Frankly, no. But every terrorist group has stories that can't be explained any other way. About ghosts, giants, goblins, genies, that sort of thing."

Our hero could not help laughing.

"You can laugh. I used to. At first. Some of the experiences I've had happened while I was fully conscious. I don't find it so easy to laugh any more."

"I'm interested. Go on."

The Beard told him about a man he had often met on dark nights. He had never been able to see him. He strongly suspected that the man was very old. They shared brief, but very serious, conversations. The old man was very deaf. Everything had to be repeated over and over. In the end he used to shout at the old man. And the old man always broke off their conversation because he felt insulted, he thought the Beard was scolding him. The old man always left, crying . . .

Our hero was stunned.

"I think I met him the night I came."

"I wouldn't be surprised. A lot of people have met him. It almost seems you can't come here unless you do meet him. At night, of course."

"You don't have a theory linking the disappearance of our

food with Banquo's ghost, do you?"

"It's possible, of course. But I don't really think it's very likely. He's too old a ghost to carry away tons of provisions on his own."

"Unless he was God."

"By normal standards, it would have taken an entire company. If they used a truck."

"And if they didn't?"

"A battalion."

"Stranger and stranger. An army patrol, or a terrorist band, of over a thousand men, here. How likely is that?"

"Not at all. They couldn't operate; that's why the district was so ideal as far as we were concerned. Even other bands called it 'the edge of the earth'. Before the war hardly anyone came here at all."

"Most peculiar."

"I was the only one left once the group decided to disband. I've never seen another soul. Except you — and the old man."

The Beard laughed.

"It seems to me you're getting further and further away from the answer to your problem."

"You're right."

Our hero nodded.

"Well, what next, Sherlock Holmes?"

They laughed.

"Starve — until our blood stops running."

"And until it does?"

"Oh all sorts of things. Play chess, or cards, chasings, sing songs, write our memoirs, poetry. Or do what the dogs did. . ."

"So you agree with me?"

"Why not? You're never alone when you agree with someone else. Especially when they believe what you believe anyway."

They lived, both of them, in that strange isolated village according to rules they drew up to enable them to live. The rules were only a small part of all possible and probable ways of life.

One of the other possible ways: follow the unpaved road back to the arms of the two women who N.B. had discovered love for the first time in their lives N.B. for our heroes.

This way was filled with the warmth and gentleness of love. There were additional benefits which the little fat man could provide. Although he was a criminal, he wanted his friends, virtue, truth, beauty, loyalty, humanity, gentleness, love.

Another way was to return to town and live like ordinary men. Marry ordinary women in the ordinary way. Get ordinary children in the ordinary way, grow old the ordinary way, and eventually die in the ordinary way and be buried in the ordinary way in an ordinary cemetery.

And there were many other ways. As many as stars in the sky. But they decided: to stay and be ordinary in their extraordinary village, and wait like ordinary men for whatever extraordinary thing might happen.

One day the Beard could no longer stand up. He had a fever. Clear liquid ran from his nose and mouth. All the time.

He tried to comfort our hero by telling him not to worry. It was quite common, under the circumstances, he said. He smiled wanly, then closed his eyes. He was dead.

"Today it's his turn. Tomorrow, it's mine," thought our hero. He wondered what to do in the meantime.

He decided not to bury the Beard. If he buried him, the Beard would be "under" the ground. Despite the smell, the Beard "above" ground was far more real and concrete.

Conversations such as had taken place in the transmigrant settlement took place again. Noisy conversations, complete with laughter, curses and arguments. And thus not monologues. And not interior monologues.

He talked with everything. The empty houses, the bare yards, the corpse, the persistent drought.

With one of them at a time, one by one, and all together.

"You're starting to stink," he said one day with a laugh, clapping his friend on the shoulder. "Lord, how soft he feels," he thought. When he examined the shoulder more closely, it was shredding. Foul flesh flowered under the skin.

"What a good friend. You can't keep anything from me,

can you?" he laughed. He wanted to avoid touching him. He needed a firm, genuine, real friend, with the appearance, body and build of a man. Not an abstract friend, an abstract human being, a "human being" in quotation marks, a human being "under" ground, a deceased person, an R.I.P. person.

He didn't want the memory of a friend, a posthumous friend, crying: "Lest we forget . . ."

As was his custom, he slept near his friend. "You can get used to anything," he thought when he realised that he could no longer smell the corpse. Everything was a matter of custom. The problem was to accustom oneself. To get used to not eating or drinking, despite the drought. If only he could get used to not dying . . . and not living . . .

One day he couldn't stand either. He felt his nose and mouth and was delighted to find that there was no liquid.

Obviously what one person does isn't necessarily what another has to do. Death is a personal matter. And personal means: different. People have different bodies and different names. Different feelings.

Because clear liquid ran from the Beard's nose and mouth when he died of starvation, it didn't mean that every single person dying of starvation in the whole world would die that way. God is very creative, there is no limit to the number of ways his creatures can die.

Although they all die for the same reason. It is required of them. Without exception. From the Pope down to the most wretched thug.

"What to do now?" he wondered with a laugh. He turned towards his friend. "A dirty, stinking ex-outlaw," he thought.

Suddenly he started. There was a noise. He tried to see what had caused it.

"A noise?"

"No. I only thought I heard a noise. I'm crazed with hunger." He laughed at the thought. "I'm crazy like a-starving-man-about-to-die-from-hunger."

He started again. The sound was closer. It sounded like a car.

"A car?" he thought, amazed. "A car coming here? Ha ha ha! That's a sure sign I'm cracking up. Seeing visions before the judgement comes."

"Imagine that!" he silently said to his friend. "A car coming here, ha ha ha."

Suddenly he felt something bitter on the tip of his tongue. "My spittle is thickening up," he thought. "I'd better get rid of it, or I'll choke."

In his mind's eye he saw himself lift his head to spit.

"Why does it feel so heavy?" he wondered.

In his mind's eye, he could see his hands clenching tightly around his neck.

"I can't do it," he thought.

He saw himself put his head back down once again. "I can't . . ."

He was shocked. He had seen it all before. The white walls, the bald head and the glasses. He had smelt that smell before: disinfectant. Humanity, hygiene.

"Damn you!" he shouted. "Leave me alone. I didn't think Gog and Magog would come to the grave in the shape of the person I most detested while I was alive."

The bald-headed man with the glasses laughed.

"(1) You still are alive. (2) I am neither Gog nor Magog. (3) I am not convinced that you detest me. Let alone detest me more than anyone else in the world."

"Where am I?"

"(1) Alive. (2) In the psychiatric ward of the general hospital. P.S. You've been here before."

"I'm not going to ask anything else."

"It is hard. I know that. Wait for a while."

He left and quickly returned with a smile on his lips and the little fat man at his side.

"It's you!"

The little fat man had mobilised his entire organisation. They finally found him in the hide-out, three-quarters dead. The two men embraced each other. Our hero cried. Howled. Doctors and nurses came running.

They left, having understood the situation perfectly, once they saw the bald-headed man with the glasses.

The little fat man cried too. The bald-headed man with the

glasses watched them cynically. Then he touched the little fat man on the shoulder and whispered something to him.

"What are you talking about?" thundered our hero. "It's not polite to whisper in front of someone else. It's downright ignorant."

The bald-headed man with the glasses flushed. He gasped. There were various words on the tip of his tongue but he swallowed them all. His eyes were big and round.

The little fat man laughed. He whispered something to our hero.

"What did you say?" roared our hero. "Why are you whispering? We're not thieves, are we? Not bandits . . ."

The words stuck in his throat.

"Bandits . . ."

He blinked. He stared at the two men.

"Where is *he*?"

"If by *he*, you mean your dead friend, . . ."

"Dead? My learned doctor, the term is 'departed' . . ."

The bald-headed man with the glasses was now a very angry bald-headed man with the glasses.

"How difficult it is for two human beings to communicate with each other," he thought, wiping the sweat from the back of his neck with a silk handkerchief. After swallowing his saliva twice, he continued in a quiet tone which held great, dramatically explosive, potential.

"If by *he*, you mean your dearly departed friend, then . . ."

". . . then he's in his grave, isn't he? That's reality twice removed. It's not true. It's the sort of thing pseudo-philosophers build around $2 \times 2 = 4$."

The bald-headed man with the glasses was shocked. Surprise, anger and bitterness boiled in his eyes. He looked ready to kill our hero. "If only there were no medical ethics!" he thought fiercely to himself.

Medical ethics forced him to swallow both his saliva and his anger. He pretended to smile.

Suddenly our hero grabbed him and the little fat man very tightly with both hands. His face was white.

"Has he been buried?"

"Now it's my turn," thought the doctor. With a voice

sharper than the sharpest razor he replied:

"Of course not. The departed leave no remains."

He was disappointed as he waited behind his thick-lensed glasses to see what effect the words would have on our hero. Our hero laughed. He roared with laughter.

"That's a reply, not an answer. It seems psychiatrists have complexes just like everyone else. Ha ha ha."

The little fat man exploded with laughter.

As they laughed at him, the bald-headed man with the glasses lost control of himself. He was angry at what he had done. How could he have created such a comic situation, which presented him as nothing more and nothing less than an absolute fool.

Normally such intrinsic anger leads to an explosion. Even in a psychiatrist.

He stormed off to the director's office. The director was a doctor who looked like Einstein.

Their discussion was short, and sharp.

"I'm only human!"

"So are we all," Einstein replied. "Enjoy your leave. I hope we meet again."

The bald-headed man with the glasses ran to his car, flew to his house, and dragged his wife to the mountains for three months "official leave".

Our hero still felt that there was nothing wrong with him. He and Einstein were both delighted when he left the hospital.

Our hero was delighted by definition. He knew that he was not sick and should not be in a hospital. The ones who were really sick were the people who had brought him there in the first place. And the doctors were the sickest of them all!

Einstein was officially happy. He was a good civil servant. Our hero's departure guaranteed that a state utility could once more be run along established lines, in a peaceable manner. And nothing is more important in these difficult days, as everyone knows.

The little fat man came to meet him.

"Where do you think you'll go?"

"I don't know."

"Will you stop being arrogant for a moment and accept a friend's kindness?"

"I can't say: I might and I mightn't."

"You bastard!!" screamed the little fat man.

He was furious.

"Why do you cheat me all the time? Why do you cheat yourself? Do you know what you really are? A mouldy imitation of certain mouldy old Greek philosophers. You behave like some lost Socrates shipwrecked among us, trying to pass your addled words off as truth. You aren't human. You're nothing but a fine-sounding echo of a philosophy book. And yet you are far smarter than anyone I know. Or you could be, if you wanted to be. But you don't! You're pleasant, but you waste yourself dreaming about what you read in a book a long time ago. Life doesn't bother you, it's for other people. You're like a tree eaten out by termites. There's a parasite gnawing you: non-being. Bullshit! You love the word, you can't stop talking about it. But if there's nothing, then there's nothing. If it isn't there, why make such a fuss about it? You're not hollow: you're full. Full!"

Our hero listened in silence as his friend raved. "He's angry at me. At last!" he thought. And he relished the dark red moment as the drought sky caught in the car window: "I always knew he was a friend. I do like him."

Right at the last corner before the little fat man's house, our hero asked him to stop the car.

"I want to get out."

"Here?"

"Yes."

He got out and stood on the footpath.

"Where will you go?"

Our hero laughed. He pinched his friend's cheek.

"I don't know," he whispered. "Thanks for everything. And . . . my regards to your wife."

"Oh, my wife . . ."

"My regards, nothing else. I'd appreciate it if you told her I'm nothing more than a worm-eaten tree."

He held his friend's hand tightly. His face and eyes were red. There were tears in the corners of his eyelids.

"Don't cry, please," said our hero. There were tears in his own eyes.

Two hands shook on behalf of two hearts and two friends, two lonely men who had decided to be friends by following different paths.

The little fat man quickly slipped something into our hero's hand.

"Please take this. It'll make your trip easier."

He flicked a tear from his cheek. His trembling hands gripped the steering wheel. He pressed the accelerator. The car flew like the very devil.

And our hero kept walking. A latter-day Don Quixote, trying to fight the windmills in his head, by walking. On and on, to the end of the road. Until he could no longer walk.

Life is a journey, he decided. From his father's sperm, to the mountain terrorist hide-out, to the grave, was one long road.

He decided to take the road to the cemetery.

"A warrior was buried here recently," he snapped at the cemetery overseer. "Where is he?"

"Damn," he thought to himself. "The state runs everything. You're not even safe when you're dead." He cursed the spreading bureaucracy.

"A warrior? You've come to the wrong place, sir. You want the Memorial Park. It's on the south side of town."

"Does the park include a cemetery?"

"That's on the north side of town."

"North from where?"

"I beg your pardon, sir?"

"Oh shut up! I don't think he'd be there anyway."

The assistant junior book-keeper quickly whispered something to the overseer.

"That's rude!" shouted our hero.

The two officials blanched.

"I don't care if we are in a cemetery, that's no excuse. It's rude to whisper in front of someone else."

The two men looked at each other anxiously.

"I think I know who you're looking for. Please follow me, sir."

"About time, sir."

He followed him in a rage.

He was shocked.

"That couldn't possibly be him!" he snapped.

The overseer had led him to a half-finished Balinese temple. Cement, sand, gravel, iron rods and other items were stacked around it. There were about twenty workmen.

"It is!" the administrator firmly replied.

Then he explained that the little fat man had arranged everything. He showed our hero the blueprint. The mausoleum was as big as a minister's house, and featured a waiting room, a kitchen and a bathroom. The floor was tiled with imported marble. The walls were made of terazzo, terra-cotta, and heaven only knew what else. They were covered with paintings, bas-reliefs, mosaics, fountains and air-conditioning units. The coffin was made of teak and edged with iron. It was placed in a vault and surrounded by four electric perpetual flames.

"Who was the architect?" our hero asked. He was nauseated.

"The greatest architect in the country."

"I don't doubt that."

Revolted and disgusted.

He wanted to run away as quickly as he could.

His eyes collided with a large marble block.

"What's that?"

"The inscription. It's to go near the gate."

"What language is it written in?"

"Sanskrit."

"What does it say?"

"I don't know."

Our hero took a crowbar from a worker and proceeded, in a highly efficient manner, to hammer at the inscription. Sanskrit letters leapt in various directions.

"What are you doing, sir?" shouted the administrator. His face was deathly pale.

"You can see exactly what I'm doing. Tell my friend, the man responsible for all this, that I insist he put up another inscription. One everyone can understand. Not in a foreign language."

He walked angrily away, cursing cultural history and every letter in the Sa-n-skri-t a-lpha-bet and the entire gra-mm-ar.

"What race am I, anyway?" he wondered.

"*A mouldy old Greek,*" snapped a voice inside him. "*A shipwrecked Socrates. A hollow log.*"

He laughed out loud.

Most societies do not consider it normal for a person to laugh on his own. A crowd soon gathered.

A policeman in a white helmet came over.

"I want to have nothing to do with you!" snapped our hero.

"Right. If it was up to me, I wouldn't want anything to do with you either. In the name of Allah, a million times no! But because I'm a policeman, because I have a wife and child at home, and because you've created the most enormous traffic jam, I don't have any choice. If you would go and laugh somewhere else, disperse the crowd and allow the traffic to flow the way that it normally does, I can only say that the state — in the person of myself — would be very grateful."

"Hm," thought our hero, "this is no ordinary policeman. By the way he speaks I'd say he was a priest or second-rate writer who — because he has a wife and child — was forced to take whatever work he could get."

"I quite understand," he said, patting the officer on the shoulder. The crowd laughed, then dispersed.

"Before this crazy town officially decides that I'm crazy, I'd better find a job."

Although he regarded tramps as an essential component in every modern city, he refused on principle to join them.

Tramps were an aspect of urbanisation. Urbanisation means the sociology of economics. Socio-economics means the belly.

Most tramps are beggars. Persistent speculators in human kindness. Skilful exploiters of God's decrees on humanitarianism, especially in relation to alms-giving. Of course not all tramps are motivated this way. Some have other motives. Motives which are part of modern life: such as restlessness, anxiety and alienation.

These latter motives do not force people into cities. The feelings are universal. A person with them could go anywhere. Including where he already was. In other words, nowhere.

The essential basis of contemporary — and historical — gypsydom is: migration. The only requirement: energy. The strength to get up and go anywhere at any time, and adjust the best one can to any possible circumstances.

The partisan is the true tramp.

The town was dry. The drought had entered the marrow of its bones, every cell. Buildings stood hard and white under the merciless sun. Roads smelt of melting asphalt. Roots cut into the sky. The sky was like the outside of an active furnace.

The inhabitants of the city carried the drought under their armpits. In their necks, bellies and on their shoulders. It was in every comma, semi-colon, full stop, colon, dash and sentence. It was in every act of sexual intercourse. In the advertising slides at the picture show, the editor's table of the daily newspaper, the mayor's briefcase. It was in the rubbish tins, the telephone wires and the Bombay bloomers worn by the ministers. The drought was everywhere.

It was not an abstract thing. It was a living creature, with long sharp claws. It could not be ignored. Like a social outcast. It demanded special attention. Absolute submission. No one was allowed to talk about anything else, not the ministers in cabinet, not the tramps whispering furtively under bridges. One had to fight over it, hate it and love it. It demanded motions, resolutions, petitions, no-confidence motions, to be accepted with acclamation, to be amended, foreshadowed, replicated and duplicated. Last of all, it insisted on being understood. Known. And forgiven.

Everything — was drought. The gloomy face of the fat woman walking along the footpath. The banana skin tossed carelessly on a street corner. The distant train whistle. The weary eagle flying in the sky. The kitten playing with its shadow at midday. The tramp baby sucking at its mother's elongated barren breast. The rich pilgrims back from Mecca, who locked themselves away all day with their young wives. These were all drought.

The drought had such an imperialistic and totalitarian hold that nobody ever thought of rain. Intellect and emotion were limited to: the drought. And beyond that: to the drought.

It was impossible to think of rain. Rain was something people remembered. And because memories are false and sentimental, as is history and psychology, but not economics, especially the economics of developing nations, nobody bothered about it.

And that was the end of the matter! Rain concerned only those involved in outer space. God, doctors of thermonuclear physics, prophets of peace and officers commanding ballistic rocket brigades.

It did not involve ordinary people N.B. those walking barefooted on melting roads of tar.

A problem? There was no problem. The drought was due to cosmic, cosmological and cosmogenic, and heaven only knew what other, factors found in part of one man's gut as he stood on one part of the earth. That happened all the time. And hence was not a problem.

The lack of vitamins, bodily distension caused by malnutrition, unnatural physical and spiritual growths, could be attributed to the origin of life: death. Compared to death, they are meaningless. Death is the final risk none of us can escape.

He met a funeral procession walking down a long straight road.

"Did the drought get him?" he asked.

"Drought? What are you talking about?"

They were angry.

"About death. The deceased — why did he die?"

They stood looking at him from his dirty toenails to his long hair and beard for a long time. Then they sighed. They turned and hurried to rejoin the rest of the procession. Once there, they shook their heads. From time to time they looked back and sighed as they thought how hard it is for human beings to communicate with each other.

He fondled the money the little fat man had given him.

"Now that I've got money, I can eat," he thought. As the first mouthfull of rice and curry passed down his throat he realised that the reverse was not necessarily true. It didn't follow that because a man needed to eat, he had money.

The kind stallholder refused to be paid.

"Keep your money. Save it for tomorrow."

"I'm coming back here tomorrow. Can I eat for nothing then too?"

The man panicked.

"You'd better take it. It's mine. By rights it's yours. You're a stallholder, aren't you. Not a charitable institution."

With a plate of curry and rice inside him, and the stall and its surprised owner behind him, he planted his feet firmly on the ground. "That's strange," thought our hero. "The sky looks different because of that plate of rice. The drought seems more tolerant."

He laughed. He was not seeing through his eyes but through his belly and a plate of rice.

He stopped in front of a shop window and admired the display. The owner — a middle aged woman — rushed out and shoved money into his hand.

"Now go away. Immediately!"

A girl at another shop greeted him coldly.

"I'm sorry!"

He stayed there, staring at himself in the glass.

"Look how my social standing has declined!" he thought.

He stared at his silhouette. It was full of dirt, rags, hunger, anxiety and loneliness.

He looked at the girl. She shivered and ran inside the shop.

"I'm sorry too!" he shouted, laughing. He left.

"Society sees me in one of two ways," he decided. "People either pity me, or they are frightened of me. Not that there's ultimately any difference. They're the same thing. You pity someone because you're frightened by him."

A car blew its horn at him. He leapt to the edge of the road. A booming laugh followed him from behind the steering wheel of the Land-Rover.

"At last I've found you!" shouted the transmigration officer in delight. (The story so far: everyone has been after him for some time. Eventually the little fat man reveals that our hero is in town. They find him.)

"What's up?"

"My boss wants to meet you."

"Tell him I'm here."

He began to walk away.

The officer chased after him.

"All right! All right! I will."

The Bureau of Meteorology had announced the glad tidings that wind and clouds were speeding towards the motherland. According to their scholarly calculations, it might even be possible to hear thunder in a month's time. It might even rain.

"So what?" our hero replied spitefully.

"Is that all you have to say: 'So what?' "

"Who cares?"

"Doesn't the word mean anything to you: 'rain'? It might rain? From the sky?"

"Let it. God is Omnipotent. He is Compassionate."

"But it means transmigration . . ."

"Hold it right there. Don't spoil the fond memories I have of you. Don't say another word."

"What shall I tell my superior officer?"

"Tell him I sent him my compliments. I hope all his plans work out fine. Good day."

He took a few steps, then turned back.

"Please remember this! I'm not a criminal. You're wasting your time trying to track me down. I insist you stop bothering me. I don't bother you. I don't bother anyone."

He left.

The official watched him go. He vanished into the net of twilight at the end of the road. Only then did he, the official, return to his vehicle.

The Land-Rover sped away.

EIGHT

The whole country was in an uproar because of the possibility of rain. In the not too distant future.

The gods in their high barbed-wire fenced meteorological observatory on Mount Olympus had released a special bulletin. Stop press news, to be relayed by telephone, telegram and telex. Ministers speaking over the radio were interrupted so that the public could be informed. The cold war, the United Nations Organisation, underground nuclear testing, were all dropped from the headlines in favour of: rain!

Man moves from one extreme to another. The scorching drought had seemed endless, now everyone wanted rain and floods.

The government felt compelled to warn those living near rivers of the potentially dangerous situation they were in. The anti-malaria squads ran in all directions, looking for ditches and insisting they be filled in at once.

People cleaned spiderwebs and dirt from their wells. Bathing drums were turned face up to the sky once more.

Drains were swept. Gardens were hoed, ready to be planted as soon as the rain fell.

The atmosphere in the town changed completely. There was a sense that something very important was about to happen. Like New Year's Day or Independence Day.

People were friendlier. Customers forgot to count their change. Merchants added a few ounces to every pound. Nobody was summoned for default of payment. Debtors and creditors shook hands in court and the judge and prosecutor were delighted. The judge adjourned all his cases and went fishing.

Everyone was happy and kept glancing at the sky . . .

But it didn't rain.

A month after the announcement had been made, there was a new form of exercise: sky-gazing, for long periods. People began to complain of sore necks. There was a tremendous demand for medicinal balsam, local balsam, imported balsam, genuine balsam, imitation balsam, genuine imitation balsam, imitation genuine imitation balsam. Balsam millionaires began to appear.

There were rumbles. They became louder and longer. They were directed at the Bureau of Meteorology.

A young bachelor of science in meteorology — newly graduated, with first class honours and the university medal — couldn't control himself. He wanted to write a reply to the letters to the editor which were published every day. His boss — an older man of many years' experience — wouldn't let him, "Silence in a thousand languages is the best defence, and the best form of attack," he said.

At the insistence of the electorate, the government and parliament became involved. There were questions from the various members of the nationalist, religious, women's and youth factions. The prime minister and his deputies came out in a cold sweat. Ministers were asked to explain how the government could allow such a "premature, inaccurate and fantastic" bulletin to be issued; they couldn't. It seemed likely that there would be a cabinet crisis.

But as their work schedules — outlined in the draft budget — could not be implemented until the rainy season began, there was little point in their resigning. They decided to sacrifice the chief meteorologist instead. What else could they do (poor man)?

The next morning there was a small item in the press that there was a new chief meteorologist. The former chief had retired. His replacement was a young graduate in meteorology, with first class honours and the university medal.

The old man never touched another book on meteorology. He hated "textbooks" and read books on religion and theosophy. When he died everyone remembered him as a very pious old man.

The situation changed again. The roads smelt of liquid tar. The air smelt of fire. People were over-sensitive again. Customers counted their change, merchants gave short-weight. Debt was mentioned in the same breath as prison and death. Prosecutors and attorneys argued bitterly about precedent, duplication and replication. Judges hated fish.

Nobody bothered about the sky. Everyone avoided looking upwards. They walked with their heads bowed, as though frightened they might see a vampire.

The wise young meteorologist advised his staff not to talk to the public. "Be careful" was the watchword. He suggested that they did not wear the bureau's symbol on their work-clothes. To do so would be like waving a red flag in front of a bull. The symbol was a flash of lightning and falling rain.

Perfect confusion was achieved one day — at noon — when there was a clap of thunder. There was not a cloud in the sky. Practically everyone leapt up and stood stock still. Then they started running, without knowing where they were running to, what they would do when they got there, or why it was better to be there rather than where they started from. After the second and third rumblings, people plucked up enough courage to look up.

Several clumps of black cloud came chasing each other from the north. The crowd cheered. It was like an aerial dog-fight.

The clouds formed into two groups. The two giants wrestled catch-as-catch-can. Grappling, separating, grabbing, parting, spinning around, looking at each other, darting, wrestling, kicking, kneeing, elbowing, boxing, punching, and so on.

One of the giants was defeated. His opponent swallowed him, like a python swallowing a pig. Finally the whole pig nestled in its belly.

The crowd cheered. There was only one cloud in the sky. A huge shadow hung over the town . . .

Lightning flashed like the spurs of fighting cocks. No one moved. They wanted to see and feel the first drops. An old man pointed out that people sometimes died from being struck by lightning. They shrugged their shoulders and laughed.

They didn't stop laughing. Not even when the man who was laughing loudest was struck by lightning. "I told you so!" screamed the old man. They laughed. The corpse lay ignored on the ground. The corpse's face was a laughing piece of charcoal.

The sky grew darker. The wind blew harder. People began to dance. To leap up and down. Old, young, men, women. The earth shook, Africa dancing in its agony.

Individuals merged into a single collectivity. Namely, the rain. The imminent rain. Under these extraordinary circumstances, everything ordinary could be put to one side.

Old men danced and cackled. Old women turned somersaults. Men embraced women who were not their wives. Women allowed themselves to be embraced by men who were not their husbands.

Nurses poked their tongues out at doctors. Book-keepers patted their managers on the belly. Students initiated their professors. Tax inspectors played riddle-me-ree with the Minister of Finance. Thieves danced candle-dances with the Justice of the Supreme Court.

When the mist fell, it was like the day of judgement. The devil seemed to own everyone. Some people jumped as high as they could and fell, bashing their brains in. Others screamed as loud as they could and were dumb for ever more. Some tore their clothes, then their faces, and were blind for ever more. Deformed. For ever more. Some chewed their fingers. And lived ever after with ten fingers minus one, ten minus two, or worse.

The day of judgement was so complete that no one noticed what was happening in the sky. As soon as the first drops of mist fell, the two giants reappeared. As if in response to the instructions of a skilled theatre director, the sky opened like a curtain on a stage. The clouds left as they had come. In pairs.

The last rumble of thunder broke. The show was over. It had been a harmonious and symmetrical performance.

The sun returned. Brighter than before. More oppressive.

The audience slowly gained consciousness. Then they noticed that their shadows were blacker, more angular. At first they were amazed. Then anxious. Then afraid. And very afraid. Finally so afraid that they began running. Running in disarray, pointing at their shadows.

The crowd broke. Everyone ran home. They locked themselves in their rooms. They were terrified of the sun and of glass. They were silent. They would not look at each other. They sat down. Stiffly. Staring stupidly all around, at nothing in particular.

The town was in chaos. Corpses piled up — with charcoal

laughing faces, playing riddle-me-ree, dancing candle-dances, obla di obli da. Houses were no longer houses. Offices were no longer offices. Coffeeshops were no longer coffeeshops. City buses were no longer city buses. Hospitals were no longer hospitals.

The streets were scattered with blood, teeth, hands, brassieres, rouge, glasses, skulls.

Everything lay in ruins. The leftovers of hysteria. The leftovers of excessive joy. Of excessive suffering.

The remnants of a bad day-dream in the middle of a long, long drought.

Only one man dared walk through the deserted city. He whistled. His two hands were thrust into his trouser pockets. A ruin walking through ruins, he decided. He whistled louder.

The tune? No one knows. Our fingers improvise on a piano, a man's heart can do the same with brightly sky-covered ruins.

His delight increased. He tiptoed through the mess, stopping here and there to talk with the jawbones, false teeth, broken ribs, little fingers, watches, brassieres, chocolate wrappers, piss pots, marriage certificates, income tax declarations, albums, police announcements, ice-chests.

Sometimes he spoke with single items. Sometimes with all of them at once. He laughed noisily as they answered at the same time.

He beat on the ice box. Taking out a thick book, he began to declaim: "*Rising ground, and on it something like an open-air latrine; a very long trench, at the end of which is a wide aperture. The whole of the back edge is thickly covered with little heaps of excrement of all sizes and degrees of freshness. A thicket behind the bench. I urinate upon the bench; a long stream of urine rinses everything clean, the patches of excrement come off easily and fall into the opening. Nevertheless, it seems as though something remained at the end.*"

He stared at the red cover of the book, then threw it to the ground with a shrill scream and danced on it until it was pulverised. Having wiped the sweat from the back of his neck, he left.

At the end of the road he was startled by something white.

"A ghost," he thought, preparing himself.

The white ghost advanced, smiling whitely.

"Oh, a priest," he said wearily, shaking the hand of the ghost who was clearly not a ghost.

"Are you still on duty?" he asked with a laugh.

The priest smiled sourly. He looked around and lifted his nose further into the air.

"It doesn't smell very nice, does it," said our hero, trying to keep the conversation alive.

Inwardly he cursed: "How hard it is for two human beings to communicate with each other!"

The priest said nothing, so our hero said nothing. He looked at the priest, the priest looked at him.

"I'll make him talk!" he thought to himself. He stared as hard as he could.

Soon the priest blinked.

"Hurray!" shouted our hero. "But watch out, Father! The devil has bigger eyes than I do."

He decided that he had finished with the priest. He bowed low — in the style known as "the Spanish bow" when he was initiated as a student — and left the priest blinking rapidly.

He sang. Out loud. What song? He didn't know. He hadn't chosen the song, it might have had something to do with Verdi and Cleopatra. He didn't care whether it was an aria, a symphony, an opus, in a major or minor scale, or which key it was in. He wanted to sing and that was all there was to it. To hell with whether he was employing a doric, Javanese *pelog*, Schoenberg, experimental or electronic scale.

He leapt around the town like a happy Peter Pan. And why not? His life had already progressed through a number of stages:

(1) In the transmigrant village, he was no one and had nothing.

(2) In the bandit hide-out, there was food and another person, the Beard.

(3) In the town, there was food and a large number of people, some living, some dead.

Everything was his. The priest — being a good priest — would not want anything, and could be ignored.

"Now what can I do?" he suddenly wondered. There was no need to dig wells or to make pots. The town water supply was adequate, despite the drought. Rationing had helped, of course.

There was plenty of food. Plenty of everything. Every possible cultural and civilised amenity. All the inhabitants had to do was live.

Three days after the mist, the town was still deserted. Our hero decided to administer it on his own.

He went to the town hall. It was empty. He went to the secretariat. He typed and ran off a brief notice, appointing himself mayor and to every other position as well, with immediate effect. Until such time as the mayor and other functionaries returned to their posts.

Then he put a copy of the stencil under the front door of each house. From time to time he read the stencil out loud. For the sake of the illiterate.

The town was still deserted a week later. The only person he had met was the priest, who lived on the edge of town.

The priest had quietly buried the bodies and fragments. According to the rites of his church, logically enough.

Our hero saw little point in protesting at these last minute "religious annexations". It didn't matter whether they had been Muslim, Protestant, Buddhist, Hindu, Jewish, Roman Catholic, Liberal Catholic, Greek Orthodox, or Atheist. Basically they had all been decently buried. They were with God. The God all religions pray to in their different ways. There are many roads to Rome.

The priest's efforts — once he had run out of corpses — to advance to the next stage of his campaign, by knocking at the doors and hearts of the living still locked in their houses, failed.

There was absolutely no response. The doors stayed tightly shut. No one spoke to him. At a few houses he was doused with hot water and doors were slammed in his face.

"Hot water!" thought our hero in delight. "Some people are still alive. Still cooking. Glory be, the town is still alive. It has a living culture and civilisation. It is not like Pompeii or its sister-city Herculaneum."

He did everything. Maintained the electrical and water supplies. Dusted the offices and factories. Swept the roads. Wound the clock in the town hall tower. Flushed all the toilets.

He was astounded that he could do so much. A Human Being (HB) is born of need and necessity, he decided, cursing himself for claiming to be all HB's, or even a quarter of all HB's.

Food and drink were distributed on democratic lines. Whoever worked, ate. The harder he worked, the more he ate.

He ate a lot. That was obvious. He became a Tarzan, just as he had been in the transmigrant village.

"An urban Tarzan!" he thought with a smile, flexing his muscles.

At the very end of the second week, the apparent population of the town increased by one. A woman.

She staggered from her house. Her face was pale. Obviously, not having seen the sun for two weeks.

Her eyes were wild like an animal's. Fierce. She seemed to be looking for something.

When she saw the priest coming, the expression in her eyes suddenly changed. She slightly raised the corners of her mouth — and let him pass. She didn't hear what he said.

It was different when she met our hero. Especially once she realised that our hero was our hero, and she was — the VIP, "wife" of the little fat man.

The meeting was rather emotional. The fact that he was built like Tarzan, or prehistoric man, did not stop her kissing him. She wanted to make up for what she had missed.

Our hero let her kiss him. "She's devouring me," he thought. "Oh well, only a mad dog would refuse fried meat when it was offered him."

He kissed her. And what a kiss! As though he wanted to wipe out his debit account in one stroke.

His hormones revived. The long congested male chemicals began to flow in their proper channels. The world was renewed.

With the renewal came anxiety. The fear that he might lose dominion over his kingdom. The kingdom of himself; situated in the world of privacy.

There was only room for one person in that world. Another person was always another person, and always one too many.

The presence of the woman put him under pressure. Insisted he choose: the world or the woman. To choose the woman meant to flee his world. It would be something he had never done before.

To choose the world meant to drive the woman away. To return to absolute solitude. The woman was tempting. She was soft. She was warm.

The suspicion that the woman really loved him only made him more confused.

Love! the word reminded him of school, girls in plaits, hair oil. There was no such thing as love. Only desire was real. And the subsequent revulsion. And humanitarianism. Only prostitutes loved all of mankind. Without exception. That they wanted something in return for their love was not unreasonable. This is the essence of love. Love has nothing to do with sociology. It is based on the highest rule in economics: do unto others as you would have them do unto you, nothing for nothing.

Only a madman would believe that Juliet wanted nothing from Romeo. Shakespeare was a poet. He had never been to Italy. He had never even been outside England. His ideas about love were the same as those of every hungry poet who has spent too long with his books.

Finally — to complete his confusion — he lost confidence in himself. He started to suspect that he loved the woman whom he suspected loved him.

He suspected so.

For the next few days he had little desire to work. The town began to run down again.

He tried to avoid her. She always found him. No matter how or where he hid.

Despite his confusion he decided to surrender to her.

She remonstrated with him. He was too passive. Too confused. He had changed. Perhaps he didn't love her any more . . .

She cried. Real tears. Wet tears.

As a child, our hero had been taught never to cry. Her tears further confused him.

He was so confused that he cried too. Warm crystal tears fell from the corners of his eyes. Wet tears.

Women respond to moistness with moistness. To crystal drops with crystal drops.

She held him tightly. Lovingly. Intimately. She took his face between her hands. And kissed him. On his lips. His nose. His chin. She ran her hands through his long hair. Her tongue was like an eel in his mouth.

With a savage scream, she threw him onto the road. Her hands worked smoothly, like a pilot whose plane has stalled in mid-air.

Our hero, who could do nothing, was even more confused. He saw a distant group of clouds in the sky. And behind them: the merciless sun.

The body of the woman and two fierce eyes.

Because nature always tends towards a state of equilibrium, school, girls in plaits, and hair oil were dismissed to their rightful place. The VIP threw herself on the asphalt with a sky-shattering scream. Slowly, but with the strength of a thousand giants, she lifted our hero's body onto her own.

He was confused. So confused that he began the reverse motions complimentary to those of the body under him.

The clouds split. And broke. Pierced by the sun.

The drought sun.

It had been predestined that the priest should pass by. On seeing the writhing mass he shut his eyes and looked away.

"Disgusting!" shouted our hero.

He was revolted. To such an extent that he stood up and shook the woman off his body. The sight of the priest embarrassed her. She pulled her skirt down. And left.

"What's disgusting?" asked the priest.

He was a mass of smiles and innocent goodwill.

"Shutting your eyes and looking the other way. Either would have been enough not to see what was happening."

"Begging your pardon, but might I ask what was happening?"

"Oh, so now you're curious, Father. You know you already

know, don't you?"

"Interesting. Most interesting. If I might ask another question, begging your pardon again: what do I already know?"

"You know why you acted so disgustingly — shutting your eyes and turning your head away."

For a long time the priest said nothing. He stared at our hero. Occasionally his eyes ran back to the spot on the road.

After his eyes had finished travelling backwards and forwards between our hero and the pavement, his bitter smile returned. He was a mass of bitter, white, innocent goodwill.

The priest wanted to run away. Our hero wouldn't let him.

"You won't get away so easily this time."

"What do you want?"

"That's usually what the laity say when they meet a priest in the street. I must be a priest among priests. Ha ha."

"Allow me to proceed please. I have a lot to do."

"I thought you'd buried all the dead and . . ."

"They die everyday — yesterday, today and tomorrow. And I am not just responsible for the dead."

"I know, I know."

"Please, I must go."

"Father, I've always wondered why you've never tried to convert me. Didn't God make me too? We have a rather unusual relationship, but I wouldn't have thought that that would stop you. I'm right here; there's no need to go all the way to Africa or New Guinea."

The priest suddenly laughed. He was a mass of clear white laughter.

"You've hit the nail right on the head. Why haven't I ever tried to convert you? It's a good question. I'll try to answer it the best I can. The church regards you as a special sort of person; it loves and fears you equally. With a single sentence you can make anything at all seem ridiculous: God, the Church, Christ, the Pope, and heaven only knows what else. We are neither unable nor unwilling to confront you. But because your life is based on antagonism and contradictoriness, we use a special approach. It helps to reduce the risk of our being ridiculed, insulted, beaten, even killed. We put you in a box marked HANDLE WITH CARE. One day we will handle you.

Don't think otherwise. The church needs people like you. Once the difficulties are resolved, your sort becomes the greatest glory of Holy Mother Church."

"Could I be a Saint?"

"You could be."

Our hero laughed. Thunderously. The priest tried to laugh. He failed. He was a mass of failed laughter.

Conscious of his failure, he left. Quickly.

Our hero did not try to stop him. He laughed more loudly.

The more he laughed the more he revealed his own loneliness. His growing loneliness.

His laughter died. He was silent.

Alone.

Very alone.

The priest's words roard in his ears. Slowly he walked along the edge of the largest sewer in the city.

"What do I believe?" he wondered. He saw his life replayed in the bare drain. A child, spending all his time in the mosque school. The feast to celebrate his having learnt to recite the Holy *Koran* by heart. A new copy of the scriptures, a new fez, a new sarong. Numerous victories in local competitions chanting the *Koran.* Learned men predicting that once he returned from Mecca and studies in Cairo, he would be a great Muslim scholar and official. CUT.

FADE IN. His high school literature teacher — a failed writer and philosopher — encouraging him to read Rabelais, Schopenhauer. Once he read Nietzsche there was no stopping him.

He began to write for his school magazine under the pen name of Zarathustra. None of his friends understood what he wrote. Their silence mocked him. "Fraud!" some of them said. The rest said: "Madman!" But his teacher was impressed. Awed. Convinced he was rearing a messiah, he set the trajectory of the boy's future reading.

The thicker the volume, the yellower the pages, the smaller the print, the happier the boy was. He wrote a paper for his senior school certificate *On 1, O and Infinity.*

The receipt showed ten out of ten for both literature and

mathematics. With the encouragement of his teacher, he enrolled in the History Department of the Faculty of Arts. He passed the preliminary and final bachelor's examination *cum laude.*

The war began. FADE OUT.

He had reached the sluice gate at the end of the sewer.

ANOTHER ANGLE LONG SHOT. What did he believe? He cared less and less about Cairo and Mecca. The outbreak of war caused the first crisis in his life. He went into the streets, dressed in a bed-sheet from his dormitory, preaching and declaring that he was Zarathustra. In German.

Soon he changed his costume. He put away the bed sheet and wore an army uniform with foreign insignia. He marched alone in the streets, shouting "Heil!" and simultaneously thrusting his right hand into the sky. People laughed at him and tried to forget the war. The army of occupation arrested him, but were forced to release him after at least ten doctors had sworn on oath that he was as healthy as they were.

Once more he went back into the streets. This time as Siddharta Gautama, the Buddha. As many of the soldiers worshipped Siddharta Gautama, he decided — at bayonet point — to be someone else. Vivekananda, Confucius, Karl Marx, Lenin, Kemal Ataturk, Abraham Lincoln, Albert Schweitzer, Albert Einstein. He played many distinguished parts.

He was arrested again. And just as quickly released. Again he was pronounced 100% sane. FADE OUT.

MEDIUM SHOT. The struggle for independence began. His strange behaviour suddenly stopped. Without saying very much, he went to the front line to fight the enemy. He was outstandingly courageous and intelligent. Promotions were showered on him, as though fired by a bren gun. Platoon commander, company commander, battalion commander, regimental commander, divisional chief of staff.

He was popular with everyone, including the enemy. There were none of our warriors they admired more. His heroism was not based on foolhardy recklessness, but on skilful use of fire-power and strategic dispersal of his troops. His bearing, behaviour and shrewdness at the conferences supervised by international commissions to determine the zone of military demarcation, was awe inspiring.

It was the genuine respect of one soldier for another.

Gradually this influenced their attitude to our armed forces and our state. It was harder to dismiss us as extremists or terrorists.

The enemy liked him so much that one of their reporters decided to interview him. The articles — based on interviews and investigation in the area under his command — were equally sensational. They presented him as a combination of Robin Hood, Captain Blood, the Count of Monte Christo and d'Artagnan. Film producers contacted the reporter immediately and bought the film rights. He was fabulously rich. But he never heard any more about his story. DISSOLVE TO.

CLOSE UP. What did he believe in? His rifle. The Revolution.

This was his religion. Kill as many men as possible, as quickly as possible, advance, win. He was completely devoted to these ceremonies. The rites were a manifestation of the history, philosophy and dogmatic basis of his belief. He practised his religion with a bren gun in his fist. Or a pistol. Or a mortar. Or a hand grenade. Or a rifle with bayonet fixed, in one to one combat.

The ceremonies were true. They were the foundation of every statement about modern society. Liberty, equality, fraternity. The greatest of these is liberty.

Whatever liberty demanded of him must be true. Legal. Good. FADE OUT.

SUPER LONG SHOT. The armed struggle came to an end. The enemy took down their flag. We ran ours up. The people cheered. Liberty! Independence! Tears flowed.

He left the mountains and returned to the city. Walked on asphalt again. Ate off a plate, with spoon and fork. Slept in a house, enjoyed electricity and running water.

What did he believe in? Anxiety. Doubt. The orderliness simply intensified his loneliness. He hated wearing ironed clothes, shining his shoes, brushing his teeth, soaping his body, using a towel. A comb, mirror and hair oil merely combined to turn his hair into a wilderness.

The day he was to be officially promoted to the rank of general — in the peace-time army — he went absent without leave. For the first time in his military career. He left a note of apology for the Officer-in-Command of the Army. In it he explained that he had decided to return to the mountains with some of his former comrades. "To find stability in an unstable world."

The Officer-in-Command of the Army shook his head. Immediately he ordered pursuit. Our hero's career as a bandit had begun.

His bandits had no grudge against the state or the government. They had helped to establish both. Their only grudge was self-centered. They could not accept peace and order any longer.

They were too old to be flexible enough to accept what the "new order" called security. They had experienced too many bitter things.

They had emptied themselves out and now they were hollow. Consumed. They were following the declining trajectory of anti-climax.

Add to this the spiritual structure of a sensitive, intelligent and talented man, and the product is the tragic hero. The sort of person demanded by Sophocles and Aeschylus. DISSOLVE TO.

MEDIUM SHOT. A fight. He was wounded. Sorry he had not been killed. Captured. Tried. Sorry he was not going to be murdered. Freed. Sent back to study. Still bearing his anxiety and alienation.

SUPER CLOSE UP. What did he believe in? Anxiety. Alienation. He still did.

The town was deserted. The sun sank head-first into the west. The orange drought gilded the town's desolation.

The wind sighed. Emptily.

The sun slowly fell. The orange focused into a single red-hot coal.

And then it was dark. The gilding turned to black.

It was night.

NINE

At the end of a month, the town returned to normal. The mayor reappeared. Followed by the other functionaries. Followed by the rest of the inhabitants.

In their closed houses they had wrestled with drought and boredom, and lost. They had, however, forgotten their nightmare about the mist. Everyone went back to work. As though nothing had happened. As though there had never been a drought. As though nothing had happened, apart from the drought . . .

Our hero's kingdom collapsed. Yet again. At the flag-raising ceremony at the town hall — symbol of normality — he wept. The tears were the catharsis of his destruction.

The VIP tried to comfort him. So did the priest. In vain. He wept harder.

Because he was so dejected, the woman told him she was pregnant. By him, of course.

Our hero was shocked. So was the priest.

"Get married!" shouted the priest.

Our hero shouted something back. He indicated, more or less, that everything was back to normal.

They didn't want to get married. He had his kingdom. She already had a companion to fill her lonely hours. The child in her womb.

"Get out of here!" shouted the priest. "Go away! Go to hell! I don't care! Do what you like. You both make me sick. Go! Go!"

The VIP wept. When she saw that our hero was unmoved and that he really did go on the last "Go!", she became hysterical.

A crowd gathered around her. A traffic policeman came over. He saw our hero in the distance and recognised him. How many centuries ago had they met? The policeman shook his head.

He took the woman — although this was not one of his duties as a traffic policeman—to the Department of Social

Welfare. The Department put the woman in a large building with an empty yard. In front of the building was a large sign on a large sign-board: "Home for Unmarried Mothers". The sign was an abbreviation of: "Home for Unmarried Mothers and Bastards."

The priest was furious. He chased after our hero like one dog after another.

"You're irresponsible!" he snapped.

"So you've decided to try and convert me at last."

"Of all the things I expected and didn't expect of you, this is the thing I least expected."

"What is?"

"Your irresponsibility towards yourself. You, with your arrogant chatter about 'consequences' and 'responsibility'."

"Am I being so inconsequential?"

"Do you mean that because of your sense of concern and responsibility, you won't marry her?"

"I do. And I want you to realise that my refusal is not meant as deliberate slap at current patterns of morality. My age no longer allows me to live the heroic life of an Antichrist or L'Immoralist. Her pregnancy is the purest, most natural thing in the world. We knew exactly what we were doing. It was a deliberate act. We were responding to the healthy instincts which are found in every healthy body. The law or the sacraments were of no concern to us. We did what we did because we were alive. We were alive because we did what we did. And now the process has moved on to the next logical and pure stage. Suddenly you insist that our deed should be sanctioned by marriage. Father, marriage is a sacrament, isn't it? It is not a sanction. It is not a law which justifies the breaking of a law. It does not make the forbidden acceptable. If I did what you want me to do, my sins — and I am sure you already think they are many — would be further increased by one. By taking part in something which did not honour marriage. Marriage is a formal institution based on a natural human instinct called love. So I would also sin by dishonouring love. And dishonouring human nature. You can accuse me of whatever you like — and you will probably be right — but I will not take part in anything which dishonours mankind, which dehumanises mankind.

Never, never! I still have my self-respect. I am what I am."

The priest's anger vanished. His eyes softened. His gorge rose as he was swallowed his spittle.

"Believe me, Reverend Father. It is not that I don't want to. I have lived with the possibility of sudden death for a long time. Why should a lesser risk worry me? The problem is one of the economics of the self. The self and its proper connection with those things which are separate from it. The world. I have a very minor role in the solar system, but I want to live in harmony with every living creature and entity, including myself. Marriage would be a personal revolution. I have been through so many revolutions that I doubt whether I would be strong enough to see that one through to its end. Every revolution has left me further tasks to complete; it takes time and effort to clear away the debris and start again. I know, because I have still not cleared away the debris from previous revolutions and I still bear the wounds sustained in those engagements. How can I start another revolution while there are so many unfinished revolutions? It has often been said that man's future civilisation will proceed from one revolution to the next. But that does not, cannot, and must not mean, from one stage of chaos to another. The only way to avoid chaos is to form a chronological understanding of revolution. One revolution after another. And not to involve ourselves in a number of revolutions at the same time. Simultaneous revolutions can only confirm the prophets of doom in their yearning for the end of all culture, all civilisation, and all history. We must never believe those pessimists!"

Our hero held out his hand.

"Goodbye, Father. I have to go on. What a strange thing! Every time I leave someone, I apologise to them. Ha ha. I never have to and, even stranger, I never want to. But if I don't, I feel haunted. If I do, I wish for ever more that I hadn't. You can interpret that how you will. I just want to say that if there is anything I have said or done . . ."

The priest quickly interrupted.

"Don't say anything, please. I understand . . ."

He shook our hero's hand. He tried to laugh. Oh, he was a mass of failed laughter all right. Sweet failure. White, innocent failure.

"Would you be angry if I told you that I hoped that God would go with you and bless you always?"

Our hero laughed. He shook his head.

"And would you be angry if I prayed for you every day from now on?"

The corners of our hero's eyes were warm. Tears ran down his cheeks. He shook his head again.

"No, dear Father. Not at all!" he whispered.

He shook the priest's hand firmly, then left. Quickly. But not very quickly.

Only after he had vanished behind the houses at the edge of the city did the priest walk away. He was a mass of pure white friendship and love. Crystal.

He walked more quickly. He could see grey giants advancing in the northern sky. The wind blew.

The world was restless. Trees, pebbles, dust, began to move. As did the bald hills in the distance.

"The drought is starting to shift," thought our hero. He quickened his pace again.

He knew. The drought — no matter how protracted it was — would end. Sometime. It could not not end. Everything has to finish. No matter what it is.

The air was changing. It felt intermediate, to two seasons, two situations. It was between-air. His lungs were full of between-air. His lungs were between-lungs. He was a between-person.

The warmth in the air was not the warmth of the drought. It was the warmth characteristic of the period of transition between drought and the wet season. It had a special closeness, the same closeness one finds in a tank of hot, moist air.

It was far more oppressive. It tears at our throats like fire at chaff. It crushes and breaks our bodies like a blue condor. It shuts every pore in our bodies.

The sky pours from our bodies in sweat. Streams out, and gives no relief. It makes us easily offended. Quick to anger.

The sweat made our hero angry too. He no longer walked. He ran.

And hence he got there very quickly. The bandit hide-out was deserted. There was no one and nothing there. The old unpainted houses stood like houses in a bad dream. The doors and windows hung open. A few banged in the wind. Some creaked. A few loose sheets of roofing iron moaned in the wind.

"How horrible!" thought our hero. "The only thing missing is Frankenstein."

He leapt up the front ladder of the house he had occupied with the Beard. He kicked the door open—and there was Frankenstein. In the shape of a very old man.

Once he had stopped shivering, he sat down and greeted him rapidly. What was he, who was he, where was he from, where was he going?

The old man's answer was concise and to the point. He lived in the district. He hadn't come from anywhere, nor was he going anywhere.

Who and what was he?

The brief, sharp answer. For maximum effect. It had to be him.

"The style is exactly the same," thought our hero, suspiciously. He wondered whether it was the old man he had met that dark night.

It had to be. The late Beard had met him, everyone had, at night. He lived in the district.

"There's no reason why I shouldn't be able to see him," he continued. "It's still the same man. He had no control over whether it was dark or not."

He had met them all. They had all met him. They said it was night time. Pitch black. As far as he was concerned any time was the same as any other time. How dark it was, didn't matter. Dark or twilight.

For our hero it was now: day. For the old man it was simply: sometime. Midday or shortly after.

"Fascinating," thought our hero.

He wondered whether the old man knew that the Beard had passed on.

"Died!" the old man said sadly. He mentioned the date — the hour, day and month.

Our hero was amazed. What a strange sense of time.

He wondered whether the old man knew who the Beard was.

The old man nodded and told him the full story.

Did the old man know who our hero was?

The old man nodded and told him the full story.

Did the old man know what had happened to him while he was last in the city?

The old man nodded and told him the full story.

Did the old man know all about the drought which had just ended, even though it hadn't rained yet?

The old man nodded and told him the full story.

"He knows everything," our hero's mind screamed. "I hope he isn't God."

Did the old man know when it would start raining?

The old man nodded and said:

"Not for a long time."

"No?"

The old man nodded and wondered whether — seeing the drought had been so long — the transition period shouldn't be just as long?

Our hero wondered whether the old man knew anything about the disappearance of the late Beard's provisions?

The old man nodded and told him the full story: he *didn't* know who had taken the food, where they had taken it, or why.

"You don't know?"

For the first time the old man shook his snow white head of hair. He bowed his face. He was embarrassed.

He had come because of the food. He wanted to meet our hero.

"To meet me?"

The old man nodded. He knew our hero would be back. He had waited a long time for him.

"Why?"

The old man invited him to look around the houses. Mystified, our hero did so. He returned with his face and voice full of surprise.

Each of the houses was full of food. More food than before, more varieties, fresher.

How did it get there? Where had it come from? Who was it for? Why?

The old man laughed. He stood. He seemed about to leave.

He was leaving.

Why? Where was he going?

Because he couldn't stand our hero asking "who, what, why" anymore. It was vulgar.

Just as he reached the bottom-most step, thunder rumbled.

The old man turned pale. He shook. He looked carefully at the sky.

Thunder rumbled a second time. And a third.

He seemed rooted to the spot. So did our hero.

A fourth rumble. The sky was very dark. The giants formed into one. A fast wind blew.

A fifth rumble. The old man could laugh again. His face was still very pale.

"Oh. Of course. Of course. I've forgotten one thing."

Our hero was determined — in the name of every god there was — not to ask another thing. He said nothing.

A sixth rumble.

"Water. You can't eat this much food without water. The wells are running again. What a mistake, forgetting to tell you that. But everyone makes mistakes. Even me. Goodbye. I don't think we'll ever meet again."

A seventh rumble. The old man vanished.

An eighth rumble. The black giants parted and ran to the south.

A ninth rumble. The sky was clear. The sun reappeared.

A tenth rumble. The drought had fully recovered. It had lost none of its majesty.

Our hero ran to the wells. They were working again. Clear cool water flowed in each of them.

When he realised one hand was scratching his head, he smacked it with the other.

"I must not ask. I must not be surprised," he snapped at himself.

L'histoire se répéter. Everything returns to its original state.

Strange? Nothing is strange.

Why? He refused to ask.

Miracles never cease. Cosmonauts who have been to other

planets still worship at Fatima. Reason is ultimately powerless.

"What shall I do?" he wondered. There was no need to make pots. He was somehow certain that the wells would never again run dry.

And if they did, he wouldn't care. He had decided to come back, whether or not there was water.

He quickly summarised his 'progress' to date: (1) The transmigration settlement; (2) the city; (3) the bandit hide-out; (4) the city; (5) the bandit hide-out, again.

His material situation had greatly improved. Without any effort on his part, the former bandit hide-out was now fully equipped. Food, water, houses, nothing to stop him living the way he wanted.

"If I'm not careful," he thought, "I could go astray." He regarded his life as a hyperbola, he was frightened of being thrown off course. He lived in a world which, while always close to being normal, was never normal.

It was not that he had any complexes about normality. Perhaps he meant something altogether different. But because there were not enough terms, because of a certain shortcoming in his semantic stock, in his mechanisms of speech, it was easiest to refer to "normality".

As far as he was concerned, normality was always abnormal. In other words, average. Mediocre. Half hearted. Not very good.

He knew of no sin greater than being average. Ordinariness was prime evidence of nature's extravagance. It ruined his patience and sorely tried his demeanour whenever he came across it.

In his opinion, normal man was to blame for every disharmony in the world. The normal man allowed the devil full rein. The devil, a genial enough creature, was God's adversary. One day Satan would gather together as many normal people as he could and try to storm heaven a second time.

"Normal" was another word for "lacking in initiative", "lacking in originality", "boring", "imitative".

Collectively, normality is a republic, a democracy or a socialist state. Any of these represent the furthest reaches of idealism. But once such a state is created, after enormous effort, states holding to other ideologies are persecuted as enemies.

The people demand a republic. The subsequent state is more totalitarian than either a monarchy or feudalism.

They demand democracy. This becomes an excuse for unlimited oppression and exploitation.

They cheer socialism because it creates a classless society. Normal people make up the largest and most powerful group, they then place themselves above everyone else and use them for their own selfish ends.

Normal man derives life's drama from words. He builds new words out of antonyms. He manipulates semantics and epistomology. His psychology is based on the moment. He speculates in fragments.

Normal man makes a doctrine from laziness, then turns it into limitless power.

The master frees the slave from his chains. The slave enrols in a literacy course, reads the encyclopaedia, kills the master who freed him, then finally declares himself a carbon-copy Nero or Caligula.

All on the excuse that it is a perfectly normal way of behaving.

The doctrine forced itself on our hero with great vigour: the bandit hide-out was empty, he was the only inhabitant, the absolute ruler.

Because he had plenty of food, there was a danger he would lose his inner dynamism. It was no longer the case that everything balanced on a razor's edge. He was like the mouse that fell into the rice barn: it would only be a matter of time before he would over-eat and die of boredom.

The only thing he could do in the barn would be to dramatise his life. Live artificially. Unnaturally. Falsely. Behave like a member of the leisure class. In brief: be bourgeois.

The bourgeois man and the aristocrat are totally different. Aristocracy of the soul is the topmost peak of the pyramid of constant struggle.

Aristocracy is the tension created by polarity. By the perpetual struggle to overthrow the usual state of affairs. The average. In brief, normality.

What could he do to stop becoming a mouse? What could he

do that didn't stink of self-dramatisation?

He had dug the well in the transmigrant village in bad faith, but as the situation could not have been otherwise, that could not be held against him.

The bad faith he had shown by filling every position in the city administration had been balanced by the benefits that had produced.

And now?

Of course he could start digging again. It was possible he might find coal or oil. He would be serving his country.

He could also, say, beautify the village. But that was exactly the problem.

When he had finished beautifying the village — and he would, one day, finish — he would have to invite other people to come and live there. This would create a demographic precedent, considering the world population explosion and the related difficulty of providing sufficient housing.

After the village became a town, it would quite likely become a centre for industry, trade, tourism and culture. And then he would have lost his realm, his private self.

On the other hand, to sit there and do nothing on the off-chance that he could keep the place all to himself, contradicted the aspirations which the abundance of material possessions created in him.

The final, crucial choice was between loss of self and boredom.

Framing the problem this way was a revolution in itself. The common opinion is that loneliness, or alienation, of necessity implies boredom. The stricter theoreticians see the two as exactly the same thing. Alienation equals boredom. Boredom equals alienation.

For the first time in his life — perhaps for the first time in human history — he had successfully separated boredom from alienation. The two meanings stood apart from each other.

He could choose boredom and follow the small unpaved road back to town. Back to civilisation. Wander from one town to another. From one position to another. From one woman to another. From one ideology to another. From one religion to another. From one university to another. From one book to another. And grow old as he did so, until at last he died.

He could choose to be himself and stay in the hideout until there was no more food. Or until someone else came. And then he would go, to preserve his separateness. Go, anywhere. Even to another town, if he had to. To a lot of other towns. The geography of isolation — like the geography of boredom — is: go anywhere, be anywhere, no matter what.

But there was another problem, which also related to bad faith. Why should he go? If alienation and boredom are universal, there is no point in going. It is the act of going which would be bad faith. The act would be false. Alienation and boredom have always existed, everywhere, and no matter what. In the beginning was: alienation and boredom.

Sadly he resurveyed his 'progress' to date. The link between his private existence and boredom had to be broken, so that he could reject pretence and self-dramatisation. Real life is not like a best-selling novel. Nor is it a collection of trivial comments based on a number of interviews and some lectures by eccentric professors of philosophy.

There is only one way to live and die: with one's real feet planted firmly on the real ground of the real world, with a real knife stuck firmly between alienation and boredom (both of which are, of course, very real). The first step necessary in forming a genuinely human society is to dramatically — and, hence, tragically — destroy the symbiotic relationship which currently exists, wait for the two to become perfectly distinct, then liquidate them one after the other, chronologically.

No matter how strong or how real the grasp of alienation and boredom were on modern society, he had to fight them. For the sake of modernity itself.

He was aware that his thinking smelt of musty morality, of the pulpit and the cassock, but there was no other way. Life had to continue. The fact that we exist insists on that. Modern, classical, romantic, absurdist, styles of life, are all possible as long as someone is still alive. Live first, then find the right label. The label doesn't matter.

The wind played with the doors, windows and roofing, putting an end to the twistings and turnings of his mind. The conclusion was obvious.

He would start with the doors, windows and loose roofing, then fix the rest of the houses. He would repaint them. Replace any boards or pillars which were loose. Repair the roofs. Build a regular and efficient system of pipes to bring the water from the wells and distribute it to the houses. Build new houses. New buildings. Schools, clinics, factories, business enterprises, art galleries, museums, libraries, universities, halls, parks and lakes, fountains, hotels, statues, expressways, airports, stadiums, swimming pools, military barracks, etc. — these would all follow.

He was suddenly seized by a new and strange passion. He trembled. His blood pounded and raced throughout his body. His heart beat like an African war drum.

Yes. He would do it. Use every ounce of strength and talent he possessed. A new era had sunk its roots deep down into him.

The drought suddenly seemed over. The air he breathed no longer smelt of a hot moist tank. The hills in the distance no longer seemed to be bald. And if they were — then they were beautiful! And if the drought was not over — it was beautiful too!

He rapidly worked out his plans. He wrote down what he would need first of all. Boards, posts, nails, paint, roofing iron, tools of trade, tradesmen, transport.

Yes. He would have to get it all ready. He would have to go to town. He would go to his friend, the little fat man.

A brief mental calculation assured him that his friend would be delighted to see him and to help. The little fat man, his dear friend, eagerly waiting for any opportunity to do something worthwhile for him, as though to compensate for the feelings aroused by his other, criminal, activities.

And if the little fat man wasn't there — if a naval patrol had shot him while he was in his speedboat — then he could still salvage his plans by going to the senior men in the Department of Transmigration.

Yes. In fact he would go to them first. He would go right away.

TEN

"Utopian!" screamed the Regional Head of the Department of Transmigration. And with that, our hero's hopes collapsed.

The Regional Head's objections were official, not personal. The selection of transmigration sites could only be done on the basis of careful and fully-considered planning. First of all, teams of experts had to carry out research and make extensive surveys.

Our hero's recommendation that the former bandit hide-out be used as a transmigrant settlement site was rather sensational and, therefore, impossible. Especially once he had explained where the site was and what it was like. The bandits had chosen the site for their general headquarters because it fitted their needs exactly. The benefits the site bestowed on them would be liabilities for a government transmigrant project.

Transmigrants are obviously not bandits. They are ordinary displaced persons. Because of socio-economic pressures in their own villages, they have allowed the government — they would allow anyone — to move them somewhere else. Anywhere.

Any region that suited bandits had to be: hell. Nowhere else would be good enough. The uglier, more isolated, more poverty-stricken the district, the better it suited them. It would not suit transmigrants.

The more he thought about it, the less the Head was able to accept our hero's proposal. Especially — this was in the file — as our hero was a drop-out in history and philosophy. "Something must have fused his logic circuits," thought the Regional Head.

He put up a counter proposal. Go back to the original settlement. The wet season was at the threshold. The bureau of meteorology couldn't be wrong twice. In a month the drought would be over. Soon it would rain.

"Go back!" said the Regional Head. Until it rained, our hero — the prodigal son — could stay with other members of the village in the department's barracks. They had all returned, one after the other, disappointed and miserable. The department fed and sheltered them day by day, while they waited for the drought to finish.

Some had not returned, of course. They had gone off to other districts. The failures had become beggars and tramps. Those who succeeded were now upwardly mobile.

And of course there were the defeatists who had, on their own initiative and at their own risk, decided to return to the villages they had first come from. They were ashamed, but there was no other way. It was better to be ashamed with one's family and friends than to starve to death somewhere else.

The Regional Head used all the knowledge and skill at his command (which was considerable, for it had got him where he was) to sway our hero's heart and mind.

He was aware that if the Department had a man like our hero in its central office, the Department might enter a new stage in its development. The Department was in a serious way. It was currently suffering hardening of the arteries. An injection of intellect, talent and character such as our hero possessed, would certainly be highly beneficial.

Its senior administrators were merely good bureaucrats, with good conduct records, possibly even men of goodwill. But a department as different as the Department of Transmigration demanded more than that.

Transmigration is a socio-economic problem. A security problem. A demographic problem. A problem of cultural stratification.

Transmigration also touches on contemporary psychology. The problems of modern anxiety and modern isolation as they concern modern man. Transmigration is a problem of: migration. It is as old as Odysseus.

Transmigration is a problem of *moving* across an increasingly narrow and empty world. Transmigration is the pull of danger and adventure from the other side of the horizon.

It requires imagination, initiative, creativity and originality to understand this. Tables, statistics, diplomas and good conduct are simply not enough. Principles derived from instruction manuals and departmental conferences cannot provide the slightest insight into the character and motivation of the transmigrant.

To understand the problem of transmigration one also needs love and forgiveness. Transmigration is a religion in its own right.

Our hero was ideal. But the Regional Head had forgotten one thing. Our hero was also a religion in his own right. He was too big to bow down to anyone else's religion.

He based himself firmly on love and forgiveness. But he demanded more than that. Only the naive would confront the modern world armed with nothing more than love and forgiveness.

Had Jesus been more militant, Golgotha would never have taken place.

Love and forgiveness are as subject to evolution as anything else. Contemporary love and forgiveness do not offer the right cheek when the left cheek is struck.

No! Contemporary love and forgiveness have to be courageous. They must return each slap with at least equal force. And that is not enough. They must seek out other cheeks and beat them first, harder. The first blow is still the most important.

The "forward" trajectory of his life to date had been a demonstration of such militancy. The special militancy of love and forgiveness. He was launched on his own migration program, outside of any state pilot project or any international organisation. Without previous research or extensive surveys. With no budget and no authorisation.

He was best able to make use of his militant love and forgiveness in the area of migration. The love and forgiveness he bore for himself — and thus for all mankind — were made explicit through his continual movement. He was always departing, always travelling, if he arrived it was only so that he could start again. His life was a perpetual beginning.

He had never involved himself with anyone or anything. He did not want to commit himself to anyone or anything. He couldn't commit himself, or ask anyone or anything to commit themselves to him. He had nothing, he was no one. There was only one aim he supported: being continually in and with something.

His story was ultimately the same as that of the Buddha.

His travels were the same as those of the man who was finally ritually crucified on Golgotha.

Well almost the same. Our hero was not as important as they were. He was not driven by a single set of teachings which he ambitiously and pretentiously insisted rule this world and the next.

Unlike them, our hero did not consider himself as, or ask other people to consider him, a divinely appointed Prophet. The practise of his religion was limited to himself. He did not gather disciples, or whatever, around him, teach them to praise him all the time, let them chew their cud and elaborate on his words.

His was a personal religion, which could only be practised privately. He did not need tom-toms, mosque drums or church bells to draw attention to it. He had his actions.

This was his militancy. The calculated, intelligent, sane, strong plan that led him to say "Go forward!" — and then actually go, forwards. Right through a hurricane. If the sky threatened to fall down. Even if he had to become Odysseus and work from the beginning for the fall of Troy.

Our hero shook his head. And with that the Regional Head of the Department of Transmigration's hopes collapsed.

"The little fat man!" thought our hero as his feet carried him in that direction.

Another beautiful woman whom he did not recognise, a second VIP, met him at the door.

VIP II told him that the little fat man had been shot. By a naval patrol, while he was in his speedboat. VIP I had gone home to her parents. She was pregnant.

Who was she? Oh, she was just filling in, until the new boss made a permanent appointment.

Who was the new leader? Oh, there wasn't one yet. It was very hard to find the right person. The sort of person they were after . . .

Who was he? Our hero smiled. A good friend of the late little fat man.

"Wait a minute!" the woman suddenly screamed. "Aren't you . . ."

Our hero nodded. The woman ran inside the house. She returned with a piece of paper in her hand. From the late little fat man. For our hero.

"He asked me to give you this the next time you came."

He accepted it with a show of indifference. Thanking her, he left.

"Gone!" his mind screamed.

He fought to hold back his tears. His whole body felt as though it had been lanced with cold steel.

The little fat man, his only friend in the whole world, was dead! Shot dead, in his speedboat, by an overzealous naval patrol with an excessive sense of duty.

The corners of his eyes trembled. There was a lump in his throat. The hairs on the nape of his neck and all over his body stood on end and shouted: The little fat man is dead!

He could hardly walk. He staggered to the edge of the road and leant against a tree. The multicoloured particles of air danced in front of his eyes shouting: The little fat man is dead!

His spittle tasted bitter. His teeth felt as though they were decayed. How could he swallow the disgust and revulsion he felt?

Swallow it, that's how. Put it with the rest of his disgust and revulsion. Who cares? The little fat man was dead!

He pressed himself tightly against the tree. No! He refused to faint. No! He refused to cry . . .

Hot tears ran down his cheeks in abundance. He sobbed. The harder he tried to stop himself, the more he wept. In the end he was aware of the futility of his action, and he took the brakes off . . .

The tears flowed. Freely. Clear, warm tears, springing from: one friend losing another, one human being losing another. And all beneath the drought sky.

Even the most honest and sincere weeping must stop sometime.

Our hero wiped his eyes. He opened the piece of paper.

The little fat man had bequeathed him his entire estate. He could collect it anytime he wanted from the public notary.

He went there.

The notary signed the documents. And asked our hero what he intended doing with such a large sum of money.

With a laugh our hero replied: "Quite a lot."

He asked the notary if he would help him buy the equipment to build a town.

The notary swallowed his surprise. Being a good notary, he always did what his customers asked as quickly and as efficiently as he could.

Our hero went and met a number of architects and building contractors. The deal was soon settled: they would build a town.

Soon trucks full of tools, raw materials and tradesmen set off for the former bandit hide-out. The unpaved road became extraordinarily busy.

It did not take the public or the government long to become interested. As though in a procession, people set out with their furniture and possessions, hoping to live in the new town.

The government was presented with a *fait accompli,* which — like every other *fait accompli* — it had no choice but to accept. The formal problems of regional development disappeared, one after the other. Past standards and customs no longer applied. Once, a site was chosen because it satisfied certain economic, social and cultural needs, people decided to live there, then they built a town. This was the classical approach to the creation of a city.

It is not the contemporary approach. Build the town first! Everything else can come later.

Despite his lack of success on earth, the first thing man wants to do when he gets to the moon is build a city.

Our hero's town was to be a proper city. With every possible facility. And most importantly: without too much talk.

The government had only to provide leadership. Because the government is the government, our hero and his assistants had only to obey. Local leadership being as good as it obviously was, obedience would be easy. Especially for anyone who regarded himself as a good citizen.

The senior officials in the Department of Transmigration were at first 100% unconvinced. Then 50% convinced. And finally 100% convinced. Particularly once they had sent an expert team to research and conduct surveys.

Our hero showed the experts the utmost respect. Because they also had the utmost respect for themselves, their task was soon completed. They quickly left. Their report could not have been briefer: everything is in order. There is no need for research and survey. In fact, it would be a nuisance.

The Department of Transmigration quickly listed the town as a new transmigration district. They sent their report to the capital at once, requesting more transmigrants as quickly as possible. And, more importantly: additional funds.

The building proceeded vigorously. Our hero asked everyone to work as hard as they could, for as many hours as possible each day. Money was no problem. He would pay well, and often. There was nothing to be afraid of: his resources were limitless.

But in the midst of their feverish activity, our hero and his assistants were suddenly afraid. They were afraid it might rain. If it rained it would take longer to finish building the town.

Our hero conferred with his assistants, who — being experts — spoke in figures. If rain did not fall, the town would be finished in three months. If rain fell, one year. Or more. The cost could be ten times as much.

Anxiously our hero peered into the sky. Black giants were gathering in the north. There had been thunder and lightning every day recently. Everything except rain. Thunder rumbled like fighting cocks growling at each other. It was as if the world were playing a daily overture before the wet season really began.

Compared to how long it takes to reach the stars, three months or one year are nothing. This was not what our hero thought. He was suddenly overpowered by the demon of urgency. He became a speed maniac.

His heart and mind were wrapped in the glow of QUICKLY.

He called his assistants. They shook their heads. No, they didn't know. Not at all. They were sorry if he was hurt because they couldn't tell him how to postpone the rain.

He was hurt. He was furious. "There must be some way!" he snapped. The experts were frightened, but they still did not know of any way.

"A nuclear bomb!" he screamed one day and ran to his jeep. (He now had a jeep.) In town, the head of the Atomic Research Institute shook his head. "The peace commissions will crucify me," he said.

"Atoms for peace?" The wise scientist shook his head. "It isn't really peace when one radioactivates the lungs of tens of thousands of our own people. And all for the sake of one small town. A very disputable town . . ."

Our hero beat on the table, smashed the door shut, and ran to his jeep. At the office of the peace commission he was also received with smiles and much shaking of the head. They knew a lot about peace, but nothing about atoms.

"You're subversive!" he shouted and ran to his jeep. He drove to the house of the late little fat man. Fortunately the late leader's right hand man — filling in, until a permanent leader was appointed — was there.

He pushed the VIP II off his lap and shook his head. Definitely not! Atom bombs were not among the things they usually smuggled. Couldn't he be of service in some other way — bazookas, for instance, jet planes, submarines, antibiotics, international mercenaries, marijuana, secret documents?

Our hero shook his head, beat on the table, smashed the door shut, ran to his jeep — and drove to HE DIDN'T KNOW WHERE.

His blood raced. He panted, aware that he could do nothing about the approaching rain. Rain was imminent, whether he liked it or not. After the drought comes rain. After night comes day. It cannot be bought off.

The polarity of forces surrounded him.

He was very aware that it would soon rain. Normally three months or one year meant nothing to him; he was used to waiting, he was used to never arriving. But, on the other hand, and at the same time, this clear strand of simple understanding was caught in a network of tangled threads. The coloured threads unravelled quickly, spread and became more and more confused.

The confused web shouted: "Not in one year! Not in three months! But now!"

As in all the legends, light was defeated by dark.

The tangled threads slowly but surely swallowed his rationality. Like a python eating a pig: first the head, then the belly, then the rest.

NOW!

He drove with his foot flat to the floor. Catching sight of his distorted face in the windscreen, he smiled. So many B-grade movies had the same end he was contemplating.

Crash into the ravine? It was so close. So easy. But was that really the best of all the possible solutions?

The trajectory of his "progress" to date scored itself across the windscreen. A cruel trajectory. The same shape as the unpaved road to the bare plateau. On this barren stunted plateau he had tried to build a town. Crazy.

That was where he belonged — up there. Despite its barrenness. The attempt — even if it was the last thing he did — was still feasible, as long as he was prepared to carry it through. It might be absurd, but not to try would also be absurd.

A truck suddenly shoved its nose around a sharp bend. A horn shrilled. Our hero turned his steering wheel as hard as he could. There was a loud crash. The jeep slammed into the truck, the truck slammed into the jeep.

Unlike a B-grade movie, nothing fell into the ravine, no one died. Good did not triumph, evil was not vanquished.

All the actors, from the star down to the bit-part players, were safe and sound. No one was even scratched.

The men in the truck cursed. When they saw who they were cursing and threatening to throw into the ravine they quickly shut up.

The boss. The eccentric millionaire who had attracted national and overseas attention through building a city as his offering to the state and the people.

They begged his pardon with many words, many smiles and much bowing.

Our hero — who had forgotten all about the incident — was angry and snapped at them — by every god in heaven — to go away. He wanted to be left alone. He would walk to the construction site. "Let's go," he called.

The labourers were astounded. He, a multimillionaire,

willing and able to walk so far?

Our hero laughed. He was not only willing and able, but he had done it many times before. "Come on!" he shouted, "let's get to work."

The truck drove away, full of eyes staring at a heart full of humility. Their proletarian minds were somewhat confused. It would take a long time to unite the workers of the world when there were such humble capitalists walking around.

For a long time our hero stared at the ravine. He could have hurtled to his death down there. If he decided to, he still could. The choice was his.

The ravine was a moment's transition — from life to death — and he had not taken advantage of it. How many other similar moments had there been in his life? Oh, lots. As many as one liked. They were everywhere.

It was pure coincidence that he had not utilised it. A coincidence he was not dead. Coincidence he was still alive.

Now he could not. That was deliberate. He had deliberately decided not to die but to live.

Deliberately? That was coincidence too.

His trajectory had been a mixture of unintentionally deliberate acts and deliberately unintentional acts. This same trajectory had propelled him onto this unpaved road beneath the drought sky.

With this paradox, all contradiction vanished. We are deliberate coincidences, and coincidentally deliberate.

Black giants queued across the sky. They came from every corner, beating their drums of war. Lightning flashed. The wind grew stronger and faster.

Rain fell. The rain everyone had waited so long for.

Our hero caught the first few drops in the palm of his hand. He drank them. An electric charge ran through him. He felt cool, fresh, very awake.

He ran, quickly. Quicker and quicker. He wanted to get to his town which was not yet a town. The town he loved. The town which would one day be a living monument to the Beard and the little fat man, the only two friends he ever had in his life. The town which would symbolise everything that was good about them, which they had never had a chance to display while they were alive.

The town which would tell future generations: there is an internal relationship between coincidence and deliberateness, between good and evil. Fundamentally both are the same thing. They are both good. Both great. Because man and all that he creates is great.

Suddenly he heard a motor cavalcade. He stood in the middle of the road. They, his assistants, were fleeing.

"Why?" snapped our drenched, hoarse hero, as he stood his ground.

"It collapsed. The whole town collapsed. The wind, the rain and the snow destroyed it."

Our hero laughed.

"Is that all? Ha ha ha. Come on, let's go back."

They grumbled. But thanks to his bark which was as fierce as the thunder itself, they went.

He was still their boss. He fed their families. Which is not to be ignored these days. It was better to face the wind than confront the modern form of hell: unemployment.

The drenched cavalcade turned around.

Our hero leapt onto a truck and stood amongst his cold astounded men.

"We have survived the drought. Why should we be afraid of a hurricane?"

"It's a disaster."

He stared at the engineer.

"I don't know whether it's a disaster or the day of judgement. But we both know how it started. The drought finished. Rain fell."

The engineer floundered. He didn't understand. And he was very wet.

"There is one thing we must all recognise. Despite your technology, you cannot stop something which should not be stopped. Nor can you make something come before it should."

"We know. But the town's destroyed."

"We will build it again. We must, if for no other reason than that we must rebuild something which has been destroyed."

They had arrived. It was true. The town had been destroyed. The wind roared. The sky boiled. The air frothed.

For a long time they were silent. Each person tried to see what he could in the world run amok.

Our hero climbed down from the truck. He wanted to know whether what he had said was true or not. He knew he had just contradicted himself.

He had destroyed the foundations of his own belief. He now had a new personal manifesto.

The rain splashed on his forehead. Its freshness spread through his body.

In order to go on, he had to understand and accept the contradiction. The contradiction was not a self-betrayal. It was a necessary part of the dialectic of his progress.

The wind picked up a beam and threw it to the ground. He lifted it and threw it away as hard as he could.

Where to? He didn't know. Nor did he care.

A new passion seized him. He rolled up his sleeves. He stretched out his hands to the men standing stiffly on the truck.

"LET'S GO!"